"For Two Cents I'd Walk Out Of Here Right Now,"

Jill said in a low, angry voice. "It would serve you right. But I'll never give everyone in this room the satisfaction of seeing the infamous Jill Benedict back down from a confrontation with the equally infamous Hunter Kincaid."

"Flattering both of us, aren't you?"

"Don't be naive, Hunter—they're waiting for a fight. Want to humor them?"

"No." Hunter's face was set in that hard, intractable expression she'd seen so often before. He grabbed a glass of champagne. "Drink that," he said, shoving it into her hand.

"Peace offering?" she asked sarcastically. "You're an optimist if you think it's going to be that easy."

"Tranquilizer. I figure with enough of them under your belt you'll calm down enough for us to talk without turning it into a war."

"There isn't enough champagne in all of France to calm me down that much."

Dear Reader:

Series and Spin-offs! Connecting characters and intriguing interconnections to make your head whirl.

In Joan Hohl's successful trilogy for Silhouette Desire— *Texas Gold* (7/86), *California Copper* (10/86), *Nevada Silver* (1/87)—Joan created a cast of characters that just wouldn't quit. You figure out how *Lady Ice* (5/87) connects. And in August, "J.B." demanded his own story—*One Tough Hombre*. In *Falcon's Flight*, coming in November, you'll learn *all* about . . .?

Annette Broadrick's *Return to Yesterday* (6/87) introduced Adam St. Clair. This August *Adam's Story* tells about the woman who saves his life—and teaches him a thing or two about love!

The six Branigan brothers appeared in Leslie Davis Guccione's *Bittersweet Harvest* (10/86) and *Still Waters* (5/87). September brings *Something in Common*, where the eldest of the strapping Irishmen finds love in unexpected places.

Midnight Rambler by Linda Barlow is in October—a special Halloween surprise, and totally unconnected to anything.

Keep an eye out for other Silhouette Desire favorites— Diana Palmer, Dixie Browning, Ann Major and Elizabeth Lowell, to name a few. You never know when secondary characters will insist on their own story. . . .

All the best,

Isabel Swift
Senior Editor & Editorial Coordinator
Silhouette Books

NAOMI HORTON
Pure Chemistry

Silhouette Desire
Published by Silhouette Books New York

America's Publisher of Contemporary Romance

SILHOUETTE BOOKS
300 East 42nd St., New York, N.Y. 10017

Copyright © 1987 by Susan Horton

ISBN: 0-373-05386-X

First Silhouette Books printing November 1987

America's Publisher of Contemporary Romance

Printed in the U.S.A.

Books by Naomi Horton

Silhouette Romance

Risk Factor #342

Silhouette Desire

Dream Builder #162
River of Dreams #236
Split Images #269
Star Light, Star Bright #302
Lady Liberty #320
No Walls Between Us #365
Pure Chemistry #386

NAOMI HORTON

was born in northern Alberta, where the winters are long and the libraries far apart. "When I'd run out of books," she says, "I'd simply create my own—entire worlds filled with people, adventure and romance. I guess it's not surprising that I'm still at it!" An engineering technologist, she presently lives in Toronto with her collection of assorted pets.

One

Someone was watching her.

For the second time that morning, Jill felt a shiver of apprehension run down her back. She turned and looked up at the trees bordering the beach, shading her eyes against the blazing Florida sun. And for the second time, there was absolutely no reason for her to feel such tension or fright. No one was there.

It was nearly noon, and everything stood out in that curious brittle clarity peculiar to the tropics—colors a little too bright, contrasts a little too sharp. The shadows under the towering Australian pines edging the sand were as dark as indigo glass, and completely empty.

You're cracking up, Jill told herself uncharitably, annoyed at finding herself still so jumpy. That phone call at breakfast must have bothered her more than she'd thought. Which was silly, considering it had been a wrong number.

Smiling humorlessly, Jill scanned the hot white beach, which ran as far as she could see to either side of her. At least that's what the muffled voice on the other end of the line had said after a pause long enough to make her say *hello* twice, her own voice sharpening with impatience.

The voice had been no more than a gruff murmur, so soft it had been all but unintelligible. And yet, for no reason at all, Jill's heart had clenched and she'd nearly dropped the receiver into a skillet of scrambled eggs. She'd whispered his name without even thinking it—half in hope, half in shocked denial—and had gone still and cold as the empty line hummed between her and whoever was at the other end. And then, softly, the caller had hung up.

There's no way he could find you, she told herself calmly, letting her gaze swiftly scan the beach again. Only a handful of people know you're here on Sanibel Island, and not one of them would give Hunter Kincaide the time of day. So relax. It wasn't him. It was just a wrong number.

But in spite of her reassurances, she found herself staring suspiciously at the people scattered up and down the beach. None of them, of course, was paying the slightest attention to her, and Jill had to smile. Her aunt had told her about the bounty of shells on Sanibel's beaches, but she hadn't believed there could be so many shells in one place until she'd actually seen it for herself. Contrary to most of the Gulf islands off Florida's coast, Sanibel and her sister island, Captiva, lay on an east-west axis, running at right angles to the prevailing winds and currents. Twelve miles of curving beach acted like a net, scooping up millions of shells borne along the sandy ocean bottom by wind and wave. In places the beach consisted of nothing but layer upon rainbow-hued layer of them, each inrushing wave carrying more shells until they lay in glittering drifts like scattered pirate treasure.

And where there were shells, Jill mused, there were shell collectors. Dozens of sunburned tourists shuffled up and down the beach in what the locals called the Sanibel Stoop, shoulders and backs bent, eyes glued to the treasures at their feet, oblivious to everything around them. Some took their collecting seriously and were loaded down with buckets, long-handled scoops and dog-eared shell guides. Others simply picked up whatever caught their fancy, caring more for beauty than Latin names or rarity as they lugged their booty in plastic bags or bulging pockets. And, Jill advised herself a trifle wryly, there wasn't a rangy, gray-eyed investigative journalist among them.

She suddenly laughed at her own fears and lifted her face to the sun, feeling the tension across her shoulders uncoil. Forget it, she told herself. It's been seven months; you're old news now. Hunter Kincaide has gone after fresher prey. Jill gave the beach another all-encompassing glance, then turned and started walking along the water's edge again.

In the deep, pine-scented shadows overlooking the beach, Hunter Kincaide relaxed.

That spur of the moment phone call this morning had been a bad idea, Hunter told himself thoughtfully as he watched the slender, dark-haired woman who he'd come down here to find. She was suspicious now, nervous of every shadow, wary of ambush. He had known better; he'd been well aware that he was jeopardizing everything, but he hadn't been able to help himself. He'd told himself that he had to know if the Jill Benedict staying at the Sea's Glory condo was the right Jill Benedict. *His* Jill Benedict. When she'd answered, it had taken every ounce of willpower to keep silent, and at the end, when she'd whispered his name, he'd nearly lost the battle. But he was too close now to risk letting her get away from him again.

He stared across the narrow band of wind-tossed sea oats to the beach where Jill was standing, back to him, nervousness apparently gone. She'd found something that interested her and he watched as she nudged it from the hard-packed sand with her toe. She bent down gracefully and picked up whatever it was, turned it curiously in her hands, then bent down again to wash it off in an incoming wave. A shell probably, Hunter decided. The damned place was littered with them. The condo unit he'd rented just down East Gulf Drive was filled with them, too—from the shell designs on the wallpaper to the loose shells filling the bases of the lamps. He'd only been here for a few hours, and he'd already seen enough seashells to last him the rest of his life.

Jill tucked her treasure into the pocket of her pale-yellow shorts and started walking again, hands in pockets, head thrown back as though she hadn't a worry in the world. Even on a crowded beach she had that aura of self-possession that had first attracted him, a lack of artifice. She was a self-contained woman, and he'd liked that. She didn't suffer fools gladly, but faced with a problem, she didn't bristle with righteous anger or brittle inflexibility, and she had a laughing disrespect for pomposity that complemented a mind like a whipsaw.

It was obvious that she'd spent a good deal of her seven month exile on this beach. She'd tanned the deep-golden russet of a true brunette and her skin gleamed like polished bronze. He gazed approvingly at the sweep of bare tanned flesh. She'd let her thick, rich-brown hair grow out so it covered her ears and drifted in casual bangs across her forehead, and the tropical sun had burnished it to a hundred shades of red and gold. And although she'd lost some weight since he'd seen her last, she looked healthy and happy.

Healthy, anyway, he amended with a painful, inward wince. He suspected it would take a lot longer than seven months for her to be really happy again.

He moved away from the rough trunk of the Australian pine where he'd been leaning. Then, tossing his jacket over his shoulder, he drew in a deep breath and stepped out of the cool shadows. The heat hit him like a physical blow and he was blinded by the dazzle of sun on sand. Apt, he brooded despondently. The last time he'd seen Jill Benedict she had wished him, with savage and heartfelt rage, to the deepest, hottest corner of hell. And with that thought still in mind, he started walking purposefully toward the tall, golden-skinned woman who had once loved him.

"Oh, look, Arthur! A lightning whelk! That lady just found a lightning whelk!"

Balanced on one knee, Jill looked up, startled by the shrill voice coming from right above her.

"Look at that, Arthur! I told you to watch where you were walking. That lady found it right where you just were!"

Plump and badly sunburned, the woman stared greedily at the big shell in Jill's hand. Jill stood up, letting her gaze rest momentarily on the large plastic bucket the woman was carrying. It was half-filled with shells and sand dollars. Arthur came puffing over, looking decidedly unhappy.

"We have enough already, Margaret," he panted, nodding at the bucket. "These are going to rot, just like last year."

Margaret gave her husband a scathing glare. "I'm going to make pictures out of them," she informed him. "Like the ones we saw yesterday, selling for twenty dollars. Twenty dollars!" She gave a snort and fastened her eyes on Jill's shell again.

It *was* a prize, Jill thought. Nearly eight inches long, it was shaped like an ice-cream cone, the top a whorled confection of brown and amber and creamy white, narrowing sharply into a long, slender tip. It was surprisingly heavy and she turned it over to watch the indignant owner pulling in its broad foot pod. The glutinous black material flowed tidily back into the shell, pulling the oval operculum, or trapdoor, snugly closed behind it. Jill smiled. *I know how you feel,* she told it silently. *I've been doing that a lot myself, lately.*

"Are you going to keep that shell?"

Jill looked at the woman, recognizing the greed in her eyes. The woman wasn't a collector, she was an acquisitor, simply wanting *more*. All the shells in the world wouldn't be enough for her. "Yes," Jill lied. She looked pointedly at the bucket hanging from the woman's fleshy hand. "There are restrictions on how many shells you can collect—only two live shells per person. You wouldn't be able to take this one anyway."

The woman's eyes narrowed. "Two of each *kind*, per person," she advised Jill haughtily. She grabbed her husband by the arm and pulled him away. "Come on, Arthur. And keep your eyes open!"

Jill sighed. There was no point in trying to argue with her, in trying to explain the environmental impact she and the thousands of other irresponsible collectors were having on Sanibel. Every year more and more live shells were picked up and carted to the far corners of the country. There they wound up in boxes on dusty closet shelves, to be thrown out in the next spring housecleaning.

Jill turned the shell in her fingers. Greed. It corrupted the purest of souls. It had been simple human greed that had seeped through the corridors of the Phoenix labs seven months ago. Like the viral infections being studied there, it had tainted everything it had touched. Not one of them had come through unscathed. And not even seven months and a thousand miles could erase the desolation she still felt when she thought of that nightmare.

"Go back home," she whispered to the shell. "Back to where it's dark and safe and no one can touch you." She flung the shell as far out into the surf as she could. "Dig in deep. And don't stick your neck out for anyone!"

"Too bad you didn't take your own advice about seven months ago," a gravelly baritone said from behind her.

Jill froze. *Impossible,* she advised herself calmly. It wouldn't be the first time she'd heard a cigarette and bourbon voice and had thought, for one wrenching instant, that he was back in her life. Then she'd turn around and see a complete stranger. In a few moments, after the stranger had determined that the sizzling anger in her eyes wasn't for him, he'd ask her out for a drink and dinner. Who knows? she added with an inward smile. Maybe this time she'd accept.

Still smiling, she turned around. And felt the blood drain from her face.

He was standing about five feet from her, loose limbed and rangy, with one thumb hooked in his leather belt. He'd loosened his tie and unbuttoned his collar in concession to the tropical heat, and he held his jacket draped over one broad shoulder. She'd once heard someone say he had the kind of face that made strong men step back and strong women fall in love. And she, God knows, had been no exception. She looked at it now and wondered how she'd ever thought him handsome: his features were too rugged and weatherworn for that. Above the gaping collar, that rough-chiseled face was unchanged from the last time she'd seen it, ravaged by too many hours of hard work, half a day's stubble and what could have been the final traces of a monumental hangover. Only his eyes had changed. They'd once burned with fierce heat, but now they gazed back at her with an infinite weariness, as though the fire had burned itself out. For some reason that possibility horrified her more than the fact that he was here, standing in front of her, waiting patiently for her to say something.

"My God," she heard herself whisper. "You look like hell." It wasn't even close to the savage, hurtful things she'd been rehearsing for months.

It obviously hadn't been what Hunter had expected, either. He blinked at her, then slowly, cautiously, his mouth curved into a faint smile. "Hangover," he said in that rusty growl of a voice as if that one word explained everything, "and a bad flight schedule. The only flight I could catch out of Toronto last night went straight through to Miami. I drove across Alligator Alley last night. Got in about four this morning."

"Toronto?" Jill echoed, wondering why she felt so calm. Shock, she decided with scientific interest. The question was, when was it going to wear off? And what would happen when it did?

"I was up there finishing off a story. Then I looked up an old buddy and we swapped lies over a bottle of Canadian Club before I caught my flight. His paper's just posted him to Jo'Berg to cover the South African mess."

"You were always good at that—the lies, I mean." That was better, Jill told herself with satisfaction as the barb struck home. There was a flicker of what she could have sworn was pain deep in those rain-gray eyes, and she smiled.

"I never lied to you, Jill." His voice was even rougher than she'd remembered.

"Like hell you never lied to me." She heard the anger rise through the words. "There wasn't a thing you said to me in those three weeks that wasn't a lie."

He stared down at her, the lines around his eyes deepening. "My God," he said, his voice no more than a whisper on the wind. "What have I done to you, Jill?"

The pain in his eyes was real. It caught Jill so by surprise that she nearly faltered, nearly walked across those intervening five feet of sand and slipped her arms around him and whispered that it didn't matter, that she loved him. Then the urge was gone, vanishing as quickly as it had appeared, leaving her stunned at how easily her own heart could betray her.

She gave a harsh laugh and turned away to stare at the horizon, shading her eyes with both hands. "Done, Kincaide? How about breaking my heart, for a start? Destroying my career, my life. What haven't you done to me?"

"Jill..."

She managed a smile and swung around to face him again, enjoying the pain in his eyes just a little too much, wanting to see more. Wanting blood, if she could get it. Damn it, he owed her blood. "Oh, don't look at me like that, Kincaide. I'm not going to go for your throat. I don't like public scenes, remember?"

"Yeah." His smile was grim. "I remember."

"That was you this morning, wasn't it. On the phone." He nodded, his expression growing even more bleak. "Why didn't you say something?"

His gaze met hers again, wary now. "I wanted to. But...somehow, there didn't seem to be a whole lot to say."

"You could have tried 'I'm sorry'!" The words sizzled between them, vibrant with anger and hurt. Her eyes burned suddenly and she blinked, taking a step toward him. "Damn you, Hunter! You could at least have said you were sorry!" She didn't even realize what she was doing until she was swinging at him. He made no move to avoid it and her open palm struck him squarely on his left cheek, the force of her blow making him stagger back a step.

Breathing heavily, Jill stared at him, her entire arm tingling. Hunter stared back, saying nothing. She wondered what had caught him off guard more: the slap or her uncharacteristic display of anger. For some reason it struck Jill as funny and to her surprise, she found herself laughing. That seemed to knock Hunter even more off balance, which pleased her, and she was relieved to discover that she hadn't entirely lost her desire for revenge after all. "Say something. Don't just stand there looking at me as though you've never seen me before."

At that, a faint smile brushed his mouth and he touched his cheek gingerly with his fingertips. "I haven't," he said with a distinct chuckle. "The Dr. Jill Benedict I knew in Chapel Hill, North Carolina, would no more have done that than she'd have stripped naked and done handsprings down the main street of Raleigh at high noon." He rubbed his cheek ruefully, his smile widening. "You should have done that seven months ago, sweetheart. God knows, you had the right."

"I should have put a stake through your heart seven months ago." Jill massaged her wrist. "What are you doing here, Kincaide?"

"Looking for you."

"Why?"

Her directness seemed to take him off guard again. He shifted uneasily, something darkening his eyes. "I thought that would be fairly obvious, Boston. Especially to a crack scientific mind like yours, all preoccupied with logic and rationality, cause and effect."

His use of his own playful nickname for her startled her. It created an intimacy she didn't want, and she knew he'd deliberately used it for exactly that reason. Just where, she

wondered, was that devious journalist's mind of his leading? Wherever it was headed, she didn't want any part of it.
"You never could give a straight answer to a straight question, could you, Kincaide? I'm a biochemist, not a mind
reader. Say what you have to say, then leave."

"If you want me to say I'm sorry, then that's part of why
I'm here. I *am* sorry, Jill. For everything that happened."

Jill stared at him, a sudden, undefinable unease running
through her. This wasn't the Hunter Kincaide she'd left in
Chapel Hill. Not the hard-driving, impatient free-lance
journalist who'd ripped into her well-ordered life like a tor-
nado, turning everything including her heart inside out.

That Hunter Kincaide would have told her with blunt,
impatient honesty that he wasn't sorry at all. That breaking
open the biggest medical research scandal in history was his
job and that if she'd been caught in the flying debris, it was
too bad, but who said life was fair? That Hunter Kincaide
never had a moment's doubt or hesitation from morning to
nightfall; he certainly wouldn't be standing there looking
weary and subdued, shoulders slumped as though holding
up the weight of the world.

It occurred to her suddenly that she didn't like the change.
The old Hunter Kincaide had been easy to hate; this newer
version, slightly uncertain, endearingly awkward, touched
something still vulnerable within her, making her feel things
she'd sworn never to feel again.

She turned away from him again to stare out over the
water. A huge stingray glided in close, snuffling along the
sand, the tips of its wide leathery wings wafting languorously. The wave receded, almost stranding it, and it thrashed
wildly to gain deeper water. For a moment, she felt the same
kind of trapped panic but fought it off.

"I'll just bet you are," she finally replied. "You got exactly what you wanted, Hunter—the hottest story of the

year, awards and accolades, maybe even a Pulitzer nomination. You nearly ruined the lives of five good research scientists, blew apart three years of hard work and put a pall of suspicion over the entire project that's probably set the cure for multiple sclerosis back five years.''

She turned to look at him, anger pulsing through her. ''How dare you say you're sorry when I know damned well that if you had it to do all over again, you wouldn't change a thing? Just what do you want from me, Hunter? You used me up and threw away whatever was left. I don't have anything that you need or want. The story's finished. So is anything you have to say to me.'' And suddenly the anger vanished, leaving nothing but a vast emptiness that ached so badly she had to blink back tears. ''Go away, Hunter. Please, just go away.''

''Damn it, Jill, I never meant to hurt you!'' He took a step toward her, his voice low and vibrant. ''That was the last thing in the world I wanted.''

Jill stared at him, willing the anger back, hatred, anything to fill the aching void where her heart had been. ''I know,'' she finally whispered, turning her back so he couldn't see her tears. It had taken her months to figure that out: It had been the story he'd been after, not her—she'd just been in the way. ''Maybe that's what hurt so much, Hunter. The fact that, in the end, you'd forgotten I was even there to *be* hurt.''

''Jill!'' It was a strangled cry of protest. ''I was trying to protect you, trying to find whatever it was that would clear your name. I thought that when the story started to break— that once the lies and cover-up started to unravel—the truth would come out and you'd be in the clear. Not . . . what happened.'' He looked down at her. ''I always knew you weren't guilty, Jill. But I was running out of time, and every way I turned I ran into a brick wall. So I sent the first article of the series in, and waited for you to deny it. I gambled that you'd start your own investigation to root out who really was falsifying the test results." He sighed then, heavily, and rubbed his eyes wearily. "Except I didn't count on your being so damned thick skulled. How was I to know that you were going to play the martyr and take the fall yourself?"

Jill felt a jolt of alarm. She looked at him, her eyes narrowed on his hollow-cheeked, stubbled face, hurts forgotten under this sudden new threat. Just what did he know? she wondered. Did he know anything, or was he just probing again, just shaking the tree to see what, if anything, fell out? It was like walking on eggs: If she denied everything he was saying, he'd see the lie in her eyes; if she agreed with him, she'd only be validating what he already suspected.

She shrugged, feigning indifference. "I got off easy, Kincaide. They burned Joan of Arc." Impatience, white-hot, flickered in his eyes, and Jill felt a little throb of satisfaction at having roused even a spark of the old Hunter Kincaide. "You still haven't told me why you're here."

"Damn it, Jill—" He caught himself with visible effort. "To talk, for one thing. We never had much time for talking after...ward. Things started happening so fast."

"Yes, they did." Jill smiled agreeably, watching the fine lines around his eyes tighten again. "And we did talk, Hunter. We said all there was to say seven months ago. So now you've made your little pilgrimage and made your apologies, why don't you just go back to Washington or wherever you're muckraking these days, and let me get on with what's left of my—"

"There's a hell of a lot that didn't get said."

"And a hell of a lot that did," she reminded him coolly.

Hunter's expression turned grim. "We did a lot of yelling, Jill, but we didn't talk much. Not about things that counted."

"Such as?"

"Such as why I wouldn't let the story die even after you begged me to. Why I couldn't compromise my professional ethics even if it meant hurting you. Maybe even losing you."

"Losing something presumes you had it to lose, Hunter. You never had me." Hunter lifted an eyebrow slightly, and to Jill's astonishment she felt herself blush. "Aside from in the most vulgar sense of the word," she allowed haughtily, at which a small, gentle smile brushed Hunter's strong mouth. "As for why you kept digging at the story after I asked you to stop—that's easy. You're Bulldog Kincaide, the man who never lets up. You had a reputation to uphold, maybe even another Pulitzer to win."

She glared up at him challengingly. "The story was big, Kincaide—one of the top privately funded research labs in the world announcing a breakthrough in viral immunology that would all but eradicate MS, Alzheimer's and heaven knows what else. We were the hit of the six o'clock news for weeks.

"But the possibility that we hadn't had a breakthrough at all, that someone on our team was falsifying test results to validate more funding, was even bigger news. I can't blame you. Digging out dirt is your job, and you're good at it. Just don't be disappointed if I don't stand up and cheer, all right? Because a lot of damned good people—innocent people—got hurt when your story hit the stands." *Because you went too far with it,* she almost added. *You were supposed to just uncover the story, not solve the damned thing!*

"I had to write it, Jill." His eyes held hers intently. "The public had a right to know what—"

"Ah, yes, the public's right to know." Jill smiled wearily. "It excuses everything, doesn't it? It must be wonderful, having a built-in guilt deflector. No matter how many lives you disrupt or destroy, you're blameless."

"Jill—!"

"It took me a long while to understand that, Hunter. That unlike most of us, men like you are somehow beyond having to account for your actions, that the end *always* justifies the means."

"Damn it, Jill," Hunter growled. "I'm not standing out here in the broiling sun with the world's worst headache, up to my ankles in wet sand, just to argue ethics with a woman who's damned near dislocated my jaw with a right hook that ought to be in a record book somewhere."

He probably hadn't meant it to be funny, Jill realized. He looked so pale and miserable that she had no doubt he was in real pain, but in spite of that, she had to laugh. "Then why *are* you out here, Hunter? Just what is it you want from me?"

"I don't want anything *from* you. I want you."

It took her a moment or two to understand, and even then she simply stared at him. "Me? What for?"

He gave a snort of laughter, scrubbing his fingers through his long, wind-tangled hair. "God Almighty, Jill! For a woman with enough letters after her name to start her own alphabet, you can be as obtuse as hell sometimes." He grinned that slow, reckless grin that used to turn her to putty, his left cheek dimpling engagingly. "I want us to be together again, Jill. Like we were in Chapel Hill. The day you walked out of that motel room and out of my life, I lost the best thing I ever had. I want it back."

It would be so easy to believe him, Jill thought. Even now, after everything that had happened, she found herself unexpectedly aching for his touch. Remembering the caress of his naked body against hers, the feel of his mouth and hands as he masterfully built want to white-hot need, the slow, rhythmic dance of flesh against flesh for what would seem like hours until they couldn't hold back any longer.

Jill suddenly realized that Hunter was watching her intently. She looked away, her entire body tingling as though his caresses had been real. "I can't believe you think it's that easy, Hunter. You can't just walk back into my life as though the past seven months never existed."

A squadron of brown pelicans glided swiftly by in tight formation, inches above the water, and Jill watched them until they vanished into the glare of sun on water. Then she turned her head to look directly at him. "You destroyed my whole world, don't you understand that? Doesn't that mean anything to you?"

"I love you, Jill," he said softly. "I realized it five minutes after you stepped out that door and closed it behind you."

Jill managed a faint smile. "Maybe you did at that, Hunter. For a while, at least. Who knows? In the long run, it doesn't matter, does it?"

Hunter's eyes narrowed, storm-gray now. "It matters, Jill. You love me, too, remember?"

Jill opened her mouth to deny it, then realized it was pointless to deny something that had been that obvious. "Yes, I guess I did. For about a week and a half, anyway, until I realized that all you were after was confirmation of your precious story." She smiled crookedly. "I suppose you're proud of that, are you? That you were so good at your job I never even suspected what was going on, even after I found you rifling my lab notes."

"I wasn't using you," he replied flatly. "I didn't even understand what was happening until after you left."

Jill's heart gave a somersault. "What do you mean, you didn't understand what was happening?" *He couldn't know,* she told herself desperately. *There was no way he could have found out.*

"Just how close to the center of things you were. I didn't even realize you were the key to my story until I'd already broken it and you were gone. I could have saved myself a lot of time and work if I'd put some effort into finding out what you knew, instead of trying to protect you."

Jill turned away, her heart pounding. Did he realize just how much of a key she was? Was he down here tidying up loose ends, or simply reminiscing? She turned and walked by him, not daring to meet his eyes, feeling his stare burning into the small of her back. She had to fight to keep from breaking into a run. "Well, it's over now. So I guess who did what to whom doesn't matter anymore."

"Jill . . ."

"Go away, Hunter. Just go away and leave me alone."

Hunter watched Jill's rigid back disappear up the beach with an inward sigh, wishing he had an aspirin. An hour ago his head had been merely aching; now it felt filled with broken glass. He heaved a deep sigh and started to follow. Why in God's name had he let Abbott talk him into those last couple of drinks last night? Why had he driven straight through from Miami instead of getting a good night's sleep before today's ordeal? Why had he insisted on following Jill down onto this inferno of a beach instead of stopping for a shower, shave and breakfast first?

No, he decided as his stomach gave a queasy heave. No breakfast. In fact, he'd be quite happy if he never ate breakfast again. He was, he decided disgustingly, getting too damned old for this kind of work. It had ruined better men than he was, and over the past years it had been doing its best to ruin him. It had destroyed his marriage, had gotten him beaten up more times than he cared to remember, shot once too often, cursed, praised, admired and hated. Now it had nearly lost him the only woman he'd ever really loved.

He smiled at that, thinking of Victoria. There had been a time when he'd thought he'd been in love with Vickie. There'd undoubtedly been a time when she'd thought she'd been in love with him. But looking back on it now, he found himself wondering if it had been love that had brought them together or simple curiosity. The cool, bored whiskey-fortune heiress and the angry young journalist with dreams of saving the world—far from a match made in heaven. The only thing they'd had in common was her daddy's bourbon. She spent it, he drank it. The marriage had lasted five years. They'd parted amiably enough, each of them already so isolated from the other that the final, legal parting had been mere formality. He'd found solace dodging bullets and firebombs in Beirut; she in a wealthy French industrialist she'd met while skiing. They hadn't seen each other in years.

And now Jill.

Hunter's shoulders sagged. The blazing heat seemed to lie across them like a weight. Guilt? If so, Hunter brooded, what was another pound or two added to the already impressive load he was carrying? He'd spent seven miserable months trying to convince himself that what he felt for Jill was no more than healthy lust, but in the end he'd had to admit defeat. He loved her. And he'd hurt her. At first he'd set out looking for her simply to say he was sorry and offer some kind of emotional support while she put her life back together. But after a while, the search for Jill Benedict had become his own private crusade, a quest more for his own salvation and healing than hers. He needed her; it was that simple.

The hard part was going to be to convince Jill that she needed *him*.

Two

___

Hunter slipped in the soft sand and swore under his breath as his ankle twisted painfully. He could feel the sweat trickle between his shoulder blades. It was difficult to believe that until eight months ago, he'd never even heard of Jill Benedict. She'd just been one of the countless brilliant young wizards working in research labs across the country, doing daily battle to find cures for the incurable. Hers was an arcane world of electron microscopes that could see into the soul of creation itself, of DNA and gene splicing, molecular medicine and hope.

He wasn't a complete stranger to that world. Over the years he'd written a number of articles on medical breakthroughs and possible cures for everything from cancer to AIDS and had discovered that his down-to-earth, jargon-free reporting style was a hit with editors and readers alike. It had been one of those editors who had set him on Jill's trail in the first place. Just chasing down a rumor, he'd said. Probably nothing to it.

The rumor, Hunter recalled all too clearly, was that a team of six biochemists in a basement lab at Phoenix Research had just found a cure for multiple sclerosis. As though that weren't enough, by isolating and identifying the ''slow'' virus that caused MS, they were well on their way to establishing the cause—and cure—for a multitude of other neurological diseases such as Alzheimer's, Parkinson's and Lou Gehrig's disease. They'd also found a possible link with rheumatoid arthritis, certain cancers and even one type of diabetes. Wondering why they hadn't tossed in a cure for the common cold for good measure, Hunter had reluctantly agreed to look into the story. But only, as he had reminded the magazine editor, because the political scene in Washington had gone into its usual pre-Christmas doldrums and he was bored silly. What the world needed, he remembered thinking on the drive down to North Carolina, was an old-fashioned Watergate-type scandal to liven things up a bit.

They'd nearly gotten it.

He'd arrived in Raleigh in time to hear a representative from Phoenix Research releasing a statement to the press confirming the rumors, and found himself in the center of a media event. Within hours, the story was on every network and front page in the country, the words miraculous and Nobel Prize being used with equal abandon.

He'd nearly decided then and there to forget the whole thing: The moment Phoenix had admitted there was a story to be written, the challenge was gone. Something he'd recognized about himself years ago was that he hated writing the easy story. That's what had once sent him to places like South Africa, Iran, the Philippines, why he'd dodged bullets in Managua and Beirut and Belfast, why he'd risked jail or worse getting one of a kind interviews. So although he should have been content to write the MS story for the science magazine editor who'd requested it and been happy that no one was shooting at him while he was doing it, he'd lost all interest in it.

He'd called the editor, who'd told him to dig around a bit. "Rumor has it," he'd told Hunter very casually, "that the six guys who came up with this hate each other's guts. That there's so much jealousy and personality conflict that the entire project is in jeopardy. Find out what you can."

Even that hadn't been enough to pique Hunter's interest. He'd written enough science stories to know that where you got brilliant minds, you got an almost automatic clash of personality and ego. The very traits that made these people so good at their jobs—the self-confidence, the aggressiveness, the impatience—made working together difficult. But it wasn't anything he hadn't seen and written about a dozen times before. It was only the fact that he didn't have anything else going that made him stay. He'd give it one day, he'd told himself. That's it.

He'd dropped his things off at the motel and had driven out to Chapel Hill, finding Phoenix Research set well off the beaten track in a lush parklike setting. Surrounded by trees and flowering shrubs, the rambling stone-and-glass building looked more like a rich man's summer retreat than one of the most advanced medical research labs in the country. And it was there that he'd seen Jill for the first time.

She'd been standing just outside the lab with her five fellow scientists, surrounded by cameras and microphones and shouting reporters, and Hunter had found himself mesmerized. Tall and poised and looking as perfectly turned out as any New York model, she'd handled the elbowing reporters and their questions with style and ease, her dark eyes shadowed by the barest hint of a smile. She'd spoken in a low, well modulated voice that brought an attentive hush over the clamoring crowd every time she opened her mouth. Unlike most medical theorists Hunter had met, she answered the questions in simple, direct layman's terms, which even the most scientifically inept reporter had been able to understand. And they'd loved her for it. By the time the six o'clock news had rolled around, Dr. Jill Benedict, biochemist extraordinaire, was everybody's darling.

Hunter winced, pausing at the top of the wide beach to catch his breath. The love affair between Jill and the public would probably have gone on forever if it hadn't been for him. If he'd been content to just write a simple story about the medical breakthrough of the decade and leave it at that. "But no," he muttered to himself as he made his way through the Australian pines to where his car was illegally parked in somebody's driveway. "No, you had to play Woodward and Bernstein right to the end."

Captivated more by Jill than by the magic she and her team had wrought, he'd decided to stay for a few more days. He spent the next day and a half trying to convince Jill that the real story wasn't the MS breakthrough but the people behind it, and another coaxing her into giving him a private interview. She'd spent that day reminding him that the discovery hadn't been hers alone, that she'd joined the team a scant ten months earlier and that if there was a story there it was with the five who'd been working on it for nearly two years. But Hunter hadn't been interested in the other five. And finally Jill had capitulated with a good-natured laugh, wondering aloud if his insistence had anything to do with the fact that she was the only woman on the team.

He hadn't denied it. And he hadn't denied, to her or to himself, that he found her incredibly attractive. She accepted this with the same amusement with which she seemed to view the entire world, and if she hadn't actively encouraged the next step in their relationship, she hadn't discouraged it, either. They'd spent three weeks together, laughing and going for long walks, talking seriously over lobster and good wine one minute and playing tag on the lawn of Phoenix Research the next.

Looking back, Hunter realized that something had drawn them together right from the start, in spite of the fact they were from different worlds. In fact they'd laughed over the differences. He, the tough war-correspondent-turned-free-lance writer whose aggressive, hard-hitting style had already won him one Pulitzer and was fast making him a legend; she the calm, methodical scientist whose low-key approach to life was the direct antithesis of his. Yet they'd fit together like two halves of a whole.

In bed, Hunter mused wistfully, as well as out of it.

As he had often during the past seven months, he found himself wondering if what had happened next would have happened at all if he'd stuck to cold showers and stayed out of Jill Benedict's bed. But at the time, it had been too late to think about journalistic objectivity. They'd been swept up in each other like leaves in a hurricane and when they'd finally tumbled into her bed, breathless with laughter and need, the entire universe had seemed to fall into place with a well oiled click of perfection.

Perfection. Hunter smiled to himself as he strode toward his car. What they'd had together *had* been perfection. Or as close to it as mortal man could ever get. Then he'd received the first phone call, and things had started to come apart.

Anonymous telephone tips were part of the business, and Hunter had learned to trust his instincts on them. Ninety out of a hundred were crank calls, fired employees trying to get back at their bosses, wives making trouble for ex-husbands, bored people with nothing better to do than waste his time. But now and again, those calls were gold.

Whoever had been on the other end of the phone that morning knew his way around Phoenix Research—that had been obvious. Knew Phoenix, and knew what Jill and her team were working on. "It's all a fraud," that quiet, angry voice had told him. "The whole damn thing's fake. They've switched lab animals, changed test results, lied at every turn. They're no nearer to finding a cure to MS than they are to finding a cure for common greed. But their time's nearly run out. The Ackertons won't give them any more money if they don't show some results, and fast."

Hunter had felt the hair rise on the back of his neck. He knew that fraud wasn't unheard of in the hallowed halls of science. Even the best universities and hospital facilities had been tainted by it. But Phoenix? Privately funded by the Ackerton family, of Ackerton Pharmaceutical fame, the Phoenix labs had a reputation for being out on the leading edge of medical research. They had the best of everything, rumor had it, from state-of-the-art equipment to an unlimited budget, and people who knew how to use both. Renegades, many of them, brilliant young research scientists who were the very best at what they did, but whose impatience with the economic and political realities of university- or government-funded labs often made them outcasts from the very field that so desperately needed them. At Phoenix they didn't have to worry about budgets and equipment allocations, funding cutbacks or project deadlines. Phoenix simply turned them loose with their science fiction machines and unlimited funds and told them to go as far as their imaginations could take them.

Jill had been one of those renegades. Phoenix had tracked her down at a midwestern research facility at the request of Dr. Preston Neals, Director of Labs at Phoenix and Jill's old friend and professor. Jill, driven half-wild at having her work thwarted at every turn because of funding restrictions, had jumped at the job offer. She'd joined one of the Phoenix teams ten months before Hunter had found her, and her name was already being spoken with awe.

He'd told her about the phone call. Expecting outraged denials and anger, he'd been surprised when she seemed to take the possibility that someone on her own team was faking research material very calmly. Too calmly, he now realized. As though she'd not only been expecting someone to start investigating the accusations, but welcomed it. And investigate it, he had. He'd spent nearly four days poking around and asking questions, trusting his gut instincts more than his scientific expertise to tell him when he found something. Test results could be faked; human emotions couldn't. Over the years he'd become an expert at spotting that slight hesitation that preceded a lie, the sudden unease when his questions got too near a raw nerve.

Jill had been distracted and uneasy for those four days, pacing her small apartment like a caged cat. When he'd finally decided he had enough proof to show that *something* funny was going on at Phoenix, she seemed more relieved than disbelieving. "Write the story," she'd challenged him. "If you really think you have proof, then write the damned story!"

He had. It hit the stands with blazing headlines, and Phoenix Research found itself in the center of another media storm, this one out for blood. An Ethics Review Committee was named to investigate Hunter's allegations and Jill seemed jubilant. But her happiness had been short-lived.

Hunter frowned. At the time, he'd been completely baffled by her behavior. Up to the point where the Ethics Committee had been named, she'd been supportive of his investigation. That in itself had puzzled him: Most scientists he knew mistrusted the press thoroughly and thought common news hounds had no business poking around in things so obviously beyond them. But he'd taken Jill's interest in his work simply as part of her growing interest in him. That's what had made her complete turnaround so unexpected. The day after the Ethics Committee had been named, she seemed surprised to discover he intended to continue his own investigations. Surprised, and horrified.

"Damn it, Jill," he remembered telling her impatiently, "people have a right to know what's going on here! That Ethics Committee isn't going to release a thing, and you know it. The entire profession will close ranks and things will be taken care of quietly. No one is ever going to know what really happened. I just think it's time the scientific and medical communities realized they're not above a public accounting."

Furious at his allegations of a professional cover-up, annoyed with him for continuing to poke around at Phoenix, Jill had told him flatly to stop. The Ethics Review Committee would take care of everything, she'd assured him. He was doing nothing now but slinging mud. Finally, she'd confronted him with an ultimatum: He could have the story, or he could have her. It was that simple.

Except it hadn't been that simple at all, Hunter recalled gloomily. He'd wanted them both and had made the mistake of thinking he could have them. Maybe his mistake had been simple arrogance. He'd had women in love with him before. He knew—or thought he knew—that a woman would tolerate behavior from her lover that she wouldn't tolerate from anyone else. So caught up in the Phoenix story he couldn't see anything else, he'd brushed her anger off with a smile and a night of lovemaking, and had told himself the storm would blow over by morning.

And that, he reminded himself pointedly, had been his second mistake. The third had been blithely lying to her the following day, telling her he wasn't going to continue poking around Phoenix when he had every intention of doing just that. The easy lie had been bad enough; the arrogance behind thinking himself justified in telling the lie unforgivable. It had taken months for him to realize the truth in what Jill had said only moments ago: that he had somehow become corrupted over the years into believing that the end story justified whatever means it took to get it. At the time, however, he was more impatient than contrite when she'd come back from a meeting unexpectedly early that afternoon to find him in her office, going through confidential personnel files on the lab computer.

They had gone back to his motel room in icy silence and when he'd tried to tell her that he had an obligation to his readers to find the truth, she'd exploded with rage. The argument had gone on for hours, and at the end Jill had stormed out of the room in tears, accusing him of having slept with her only to gain access to her computer and notes.

He should have gone after her right then—he saw that now. But he hadn't. Instead, he'd written the next two installments of his story in a white heat, spraying accusations and suspicion like random gunfire hoping to hit a solid target. Jill had been in the direct line of fire. He'd known that when he'd written the story, but he'd decided to take the risk of a broadside attack anyway, telling himself that Jill's innocence would protect her while the real culprit was smoked out.

But what had happened next was a nightmare. Jill—the woman he was trying to protect, the woman he finally realized he loved—had taken the blame herself. He'd expected her to protest, to come out in indignant support of her own innocence. But she hadn't said a thing. No confession, no denial. And her silence, to a press whose taste for blood had already been whetted, was as good as a signed admission of guilt. They'd crucified her. And he'd had to watch, unable to help, silently pleading with her to defend herself against an attack he'd triggered as certainly as if he'd led the charge on horseback.

When the storm had blown out, he knew two things: that Jill Benedict was innocent, and that he wouldn't rest until he had cleared her name. And to do that, he was going to have to find out who she was protecting. And why.

"You got a phone call." It was Kathy Fischer's voice, and Jill paused by the door of the inner office and popped her head in. Kathy looked up from her typing, frowning, then stopped the dictaphone and pulled the earphones off. "Would you listen to this and tell me if our Dr. Brett Douglass is saying what I think he's saying?" She held the earphones out to Jill, then rewound the tape briefly. "It sounds like—" Her gamin face broke into a grin. "Well, it's not a word I usually associate with alligators."

Jill perched on the corner of the desk and slipped the earphones on, and Kathy said, "It's right after the bit about how their heart rate drops to three beats a minute during hibernation. He talks about spring courtship, and how a female 'gator sometimes kills a bull she doesn't fancy. Then he says—well, you tell *me* what he says." She turned on the tape, watching Jill's face expectantly.

Jill listened to the happy-go-lucky voice of Brett Douglass, veterinarian, conservationist and dedicated bachelor, as he described the hibernation cycle of the Florida alligator. When he started discussing courtship rituals, Jill listened carefully, then her eyes widened and she gave a gasp of laughter at Brett's straightforward Anglo-Saxon description of the actual mating procedure. Still laughing, she slipped the earphones off and handed them back to Kathy. "Yep, that's our Brett. Never one to waste two syllables when one will do."

Kathy's freckled nose wrinkled. "And I'm supposed to put *that* word in this report to the Florida Conservation people?"

"I suspect they've heard it before," Jill told her dryly, "but maybe you'd better stick with 'mate.' Did you say I got a telephone call while I was out?"

"Two actually." Kathy rummaged through the clutter on her desk, found a scrap of paper and held it out. "That first one was from Dr. Sebastian up at Stanford. Said he had the test results for DNA irregularities on that cell sample you sent up to him, and would call back tomorrow. Said you are *not* to call him." Kathy gave her a dark look. "Hypocrite."

Jill smiled. "I'm tainted, Kathy. Being touched by scandal's like being touched by bubonic plague in this business. People are afraid to get too close in case they catch it. Sam Sebastian's a good friend, but he's got his own career and reputation to think about. If someone discovered he's not only talking to Jill Benedict but actually using university-funded equipment to run tests for her, he'd be tarred and feathered."

Kathy gave a sniff to indicate her opinion of Sam Sebastian and his professional reputation. "I still say he's a hypocrite. Besides, the Ethics Review Committee hasn't ruled one way or the other on that Phoenix thing yet."

"You know as well as I do what the decision is going to be," Jill said gently. "Guilty of fraud with intent to deceive. The media's backed them into a corner, Kath. With all the publicity, the Committee has to come out with a guilty ruling for political reasons. They have to look as though they're doing something."

"They could go out and find who *was* guilty."

"Kathy, I've told you that—"

"I don't care what you've told us, Jill." Kathy looked up at her evenly. "You weren't guilty of switching test animals or fiddling numbers in that computer. You know it, I know it, and Brett knows it. And so do a lot of other people. I don't know why you're covering up for whoever *did* do it, but I wish you'd reconsider. You're too good a scientist to spend the rest of your life inoculating raccoons and counting turtle eggs."

Jill laughed as she slipped off the desk, familiar with Kathy's refusal to believe what she'd been told about the Phoenix scandal, but unworried by it. Kathy's doubts weren't a threat. No more than were Brett's, nor those of a dozen other people who'd supported her during the nightmare of the last seven months. None of them was in a position to cause trouble by asking the right questions of the right people. Those who were familiar enough with the workings of her world to cause trouble were either too nervous of their own reputations to risk guilt by association, or secretly rejoicing in seeing her brought down.

"And the second call?"

"A man." Kathy frowned, trying to decipher her own hasty handwriting. "He wouldn't leave his name, just asked if you were here. I told him you always took a walk on the beach at lunch, and he asked when you'd be back. When I asked him what he wanted, he wouldn't say."

Jill's eyes narrowed. "What time was this? Can you describe his voice?"

"A couple of minutes after eleven. You'd just gone out the door. And he had a husky voice, deep and kind of—" Kathy grinned suddenly, her eyes sparkling "—sexy. Like he'd sat up all night smokin' cigarettes and drinkin' bad whiskey."

Jill smiled at Kathy's feigned southern drawl and the country and western lyrics. But underneath she didn't feel like smiling. Kincaide. That's how he'd found her, the conniving devil. She frowned. But why? Why now, after seven months of silence? If he'd really wanted to find her after she'd left Chapel Hill, it wouldn't have taken him that long. The man was an expert at tracking down things that didn't want to be found, at prying the lid off stories that didn't want to be told. He was called The Hunter among editors and admirers; Bulldog among those who'd tried, unsuccessfully, to shake him off the trail of a story. She'd called him a couple of things herself that couldn't have been printed in a family newspaper.

But one thing was certain: Kincaide hadn't turned up on Sanibel to relax in the sun. He could be trouble. If he had come down here just to assuage an unexpected streak of guilt, that was one thing. But if he was serious about trying to prove her innocence, if he really did believe that she knew more about the scandal at the Phoenix labs than she'd let on, he could ruin everything.

"Damn it," she whispered fiercely, "why couldn't he just let well enough alone!" She realized that Kathy was watching her curiously. She smiled with what she hoped was the right amount of casualness. "Reporter."

It was all she needed to say. Kathy's eyes darkened with wrath. "God, I hate those guys! The story's over. You left Phoenix in disgrace and the Ethics Review Committee is fitting you for a noose. What more do they want?"

"All the dirty little details."

Kathy shuddered. "They're disgusting! Like vultures, always picking through stuff that's dead."

And Jill, in spite of her unease at Hunter's unexpected appearance, had to laugh at Kathy's indignation. Hunter, a vulture? More like a sea osprey, riding the air currents until he spotted prey, then rocketing down for the kill without so much as a whisper of warning. She frowned thoughtfully, then, knowing that Kathy was still watching her, she pulled a small red-banded Lion's Paw shell out of her pocket and dropped it into the large glass jar on the corner of Kathy's desk. It was nearly filled with hundreds of small brightly colored shells. *"Lyropecten nodosus,"* she said with a smile, giving the jar a shake to settle the shells. "It looks like we've caught a rainbow and put a lid on it, doesn't it?"

Kathy laughed, anger forgotten. "You're such a romantic! All Brett sees is a jar full of shells. He keeps telling me that I'm upsetting the balance of nature by sending these up to Granny for Christmas. Quote—if God had intended her to have seashells, He'd have put Iowa on the ocean—unquote."

"Brett's got the soul of a stone. It's a great Christmas gift, and your grandmother's going to love it. All she'll have to do is take the lid off and inhale that salty sea smell, and she'll think she's down here with you."

"Next winter," Kathy said with a fond smile. "Jack will have his degree and be working by then, and we'll be able to afford to bring her down to paradise for a couple of months."

Jill nodded, looking out the big front window that overlooked the Gulf of Mexico. The view was postcard perfect, framed by palm fronds and white sand, yet it brought her little joy. Odd, she thought, how one's perspective changed. Seven months ago she'd have given anything to wander barefoot in paradise and watch time go by. But she'd been down here for five months now, and paradise was starting to feel like any other prison.

No brooding, she reminded herself firmly. You made a decision, now you're going to live with it. There could be worse places to spend exile. "Back to work," she said aloud, smiling at Kathy. "Brett back from lunch?"

"He never went. Someone brought in a hooked pelican, Iris Carruthers's cat swallowed a ball of yarn and one of the gardeners at the Brazilian Pepper condos cornered a six foot 'gator in the supply shed."

"For pity's sake, why didn't you call me back? I'm no veterinarian, but I've got two good hands."

"Brett said you needed the stroll in the sun more than he needed the help."

"Brett needs his head examined," Jill replied not unkindly as she headed for the door. "I wish you two would stop treating me like an invalid aunt. I'm just a defrocked, out of work biochemist." But Kathy just smiled in reply, and Jill shook her head as she left Kathy's small office and walked down the broad corridor toward the back of the building.

Brett Douglass' veterinary practice was housed in what had once been a church, although the only clue to its previous life were the two stained glass windows in what was now a spacious, modern surgery. The room was glowing with rainbowed light and Jill paused to admire the windows for a moment, not wanting to disturb Brett. Dressed in pale-green coveralls and a face mask, he was leaning over the high stainless steel operating table, frowning in concentration as he worked on a motionless furry gray form.

He nodded decisively after a moment, then straightened and stretched, tossing his instruments into a bowl with a clatter. His eyes warmed with pleasure when he saw Jill and he pulled his mask down, grinning broadly. "Hi, beautiful."

"Hi, yourself." Jill's spirits soared, and she grinned comfortably as she strolled toward the table. Brett Douglass liked women. And women, Jill had soon discovered, liked Brett Douglass. For good reason: Bright and funny and outrageously good-looking, he was also well traveled and well-read, a college football hero who stayed in shape surfing and jogging, and a dedicated veterinarian and conservationist who loved fast cars, fine wine and romantic interludes on his sailboat. He was also perfectly honest, and right from the beginning had made it clear that he found Jill attractive, desirable, and that he wanted to take her to bed.

Jill had been startled but not particularly offended by his bluntness, and Brett, taking her refusal with good-natured regret, had promptly offered her a job instead. To her own surprise she'd accepted. Wading around mangrove swamps counting egret eggs and taking cell samples from uncooperative alligators was a far cry from her work at Phoenix, but it filled her hours and kept her from thinking too much.

"Sebastian's completed the scans on those last samples I sent him." She gazed down at the half-grown cat stretched out on the operating table, fighting an urge to reach out and stroke it. "Poor little thing. What happened?"

Impatience glowed on Brett's handsome face as he untied his face mask and pulled it off. He gave his head a jerk toward a small bowl beside the table filled with what looked like sopping wet socks. "Swallowed a zillion feet of knitting wool. I've told that woman six dozen times not to let her cats play with yarn. I've even drawn her pictures of the barbs on a cat's tongue and explained that when they start swallowing something, they have to keep swallowing until it's gone." He gave his head a shake of disgust and stripped off his thin rubber gloves, flinging them down. "It got all tangled around, of course, and I had to operate. Took enough yarn out of him to knit jerseys for a football team."

"Is he going to be all right?"

"He's in better shape than I am." Brett held up his left hand and grinned. "The little guy got me good before I got a sedative into him."

His hand looked as though he'd caught it in the business end of a chain saw, and Jill drew in her breath. "Good grief! Did you wash it with antiseptic? And give yourself a tetanus shot? And—" She stopped abruptly and laughed. "Sorry, *Doctor* Douglass. I forget you take this sort of thing in stride."

"Actually, there is something you can do for me." He peeled off the coverall and tossed it aside.

"Name it."

Brett's face broke into an outrageous grin as he walked around the end of the table toward her. "Kiss me."

"You lecher!" Jill's laughter pealed through the room.

"Lecher, nothing," he protested, catching her in his arms and swinging her against him. "It's been proved that kissing helps promote the healing process. It increases the flow of hormones, which in turn—"

"Your hormones flow at a high enough rate already," Jill told him dryly. But she didn't protest when Brett gently brushed her lips with his, and she found herself relaxing and wondering why she didn't simply give in to both sets of hormones once and for all and let things take their natural course. A relationship with Brett would be as honest and uncomplicated as the man himself, and that's what she needed right now. They liked and respected each other. Neither of them would expect more from the other than what was there already: tenderness, caring, consideration. And they'd undoubtedly be good together. So why did she feel a part of her drawing away when he put his arms around her, a little inward pang when he kissed her that felt suspiciously like disappointment?

Unbidden, the memory of Hunter came to mind and she found herself remembering the afternoon they'd gotten lost on a shady little back road. They'd pulled off into an un-used track and had made love in the car like a pair of teen-agers, giggling with the utter madness of it as they'd struggled with the intricacies of clothing and steering wheel and narrow seats. They'd spent nearly an hour there, and when they left she'd been deliciously contented and Hunter had been smiling all the way back to Chapel Hill.

Jill forced the thoughts away angrily and without even thinking about what she was doing, she slipped her arms around Brett's neck and kissed him back. Brett responded instantly and Jill regretted the whim almost as swiftly as she'd succumbed to it.

Three

To Jill's relief, Brett must have sensed her sudden change of mood. He drew his mouth from hers and regretfully let her slide out of his arms. "Thought my luck had changed there for a minute," he teased gently. "Second thoughts?"

"Brett, I . . . I'm . . ."

"Shut up, Jill," he said easily, laughter warming the words. "You're still in knots over him, aren't you?" When Jill didn't answer, he chuckled. "I don't know who I was substituting for just then, but he must be some kind of a guy to have you still walking into walls after all this time."

"He . . . was." Jill drew in a deep breath and looked up at Brett, smiling ruefully. "Thanks—for not letting me make a complete fool of myself, I mean. You're really some kind of a guy yourself, you know that?"

"Perseverant as hell, too," he assured her with a laugh. "When you finally get this guy out of your system, I intend to be there front and center. I'd like first refusal, remember."

Jill had to laugh. "First refusal, I promise."

"Just don't waste too much of your time grieving over the guy, honey. Most men aren't worth it, believe me."

"The voice of wisdom," Jill teased with a chuckle. She thought of Hunter again, of the long, relaxed hours of laughter and conversation and closeness they'd shared. There had never been anyone before or since who'd made her feel so happy or complete, and the emptiness had gotten deeper and colder over the passing months, instead of healing as everyone told her would happen. Even now, there was a part of her that wanted to go to him. Even now.

Surely to God, she thought despairingly, I can't still be in love with the wretched man!

"Hey, you in there?"

Jill blinked, finding a pair of deep-blue eyes gazing worriedly into hers. She smiled, nodding. "Sorry. I was just thinking about something."

"I'm going to need a hand with that pelican in a couple of minutes." Brett eased the unconscious cat into a waiting cage, pausing to check it before closing the door. "Then I've got a date with a 'gator at four. Some idiot over at the Brazilian Pepper trapped it in a toolshed and doesn't know what to do with it." He shook his head at the universal stupidity of his fellow man. "I'll tell you, some days I don't know why I bother. If I had any brains I'd dump this poor excuse for a veterinarian practice, stock up the larder on the *Sweet Retreat* and set sail for far horizons. Want to come?"

"Sure." Jill smiled at Brett's daily threat to give up what he loved most in life to become a sailor, knowing the *Sweet Retreat* would never go farther than the occasional Caribbean island. "Still free for Nancy's party tonight?"

"Absolutely." Brett nodded toward the door leading out into the backyard where the orphaned and injured wild animals were housed. "That pelican's out here with the rest of them. Want to help?"

Jill was already reaching for the wire cutters and heavy leather gloves they used to take fishhooks out of the all too numerous seabirds that got brought in. "Drop by my place around seven, and we can have a drink before we go to Nancy's."

Brett looked at her in surprise. "You serious?"

Jill smiled. It had become a game between them that Brett would invite himself over for a drink nearly every night, and she'd turn him down. "Just a drink, cowboy."

Brett held the door open for her, grinning broadly. "It's a start. One of these days you're going to realize what you've been passing up all these months and decide I'm not such a bad catch after all."

"If you were remotely interested in being caught, Brett Douglass, you'd be on somebody's trophy wall by now. The only reason you're so brave around me is because you know you're safe."

Her gibe didn't seem to bother Brett. He laughed and dropped his arm across her shoulders as they walked into the backyard. "You mean the same way you know I'm a fairly safe date for the party tonight?" he teased. "I've told you before, beautiful. If you want somebody to talk to some evening, or if you just need a shoulder to cry on, I can be over in ten minutes."

"I thought doctors didn't make house calls."

"We've been known to make an exception now and again." He looked down at her. "I'm serious, Jill. Something's bothering you—I can see it in your eyes. I'm here if you need me."

Jill stopped and stood on her toes to plant a warm kiss on his cheek. "It's nothing serious, Brett. Just an echo from the past. I'll be all right."

He gave a skeptical grunt but didn't press her. They gently took the snared pelican from the small holding cage and proceeded to cut the coils of filament fishing line from around it. Luckily, whoever had hooked it had been conscientious enough to get it ashore and to the preserve before the pelican's struggles had tightened the line to the point where feathers or ligaments had been damaged. Jill held it tightly as Brett examined the two barbed fishhooks embedded in the leathery pouch, smiling with relief as he expertly nipped the barbs off and worked them free.

She hadn't been so lucky, she mused. She'd been ensnared as thoroughly as this pelican, tangled in an unbreakable web of lies and deceit that tightened with every move she'd made. There had been barbs in that web, too, ready to hook her at every turn, some of them cutting so deep she doubted she'd ever be free of the hurt. But unlike this pelican, she had nowhere to turn.

"Okay, he's clean." Brett tossed the wire cutters aside, deftly avoiding a slash of the bird's big beak. "But let's hang onto him overnight to make sure that wing's all right." He patted the flat brown head. "Stay away from the fishing pier from now on, old fella. Eating bait might be easier than catching it on the fin, but all you're going to get is a mouthful of hook and a whole lot of cussing from the guy on the other end of the line."

Jill released the bird into one of the big, well-fenced holding cages. It staggered away with an indignant squawk, shaking its head and eyeing them mistrustfully. "Go," she whispered at it. "Stay free."

With the lights out, it was easier to pretend he wasn't alone. It was a trick he'd learned as a child, and over the

years he'd gotten very good at it. There were times when he
hadn't needed to pretend, of course. That first year with
Vickie, followed by forgettable women. Then those three
weeks with Jill when he'd rediscovered feelings he'd all but
forgotten.

And afterward, the loneliness. The same feeling of desperate aloneness he'd had after his parents had been killed,
the desolation after his grandparents died a few years later.
A woman had once told him that his inability to form close
relationships was based on his terror of abandonment. He
hadn't believed it at the time, but he'd been thinking about
it a lot lately. Because that cold sense of aloneness, of being
the only soul alive in the universe, had never been this bad
before. So bad he ached with it day and night and the fight
to blot it out with hard work was getting harder and harder.

Hunter kept his eyes firmly closed. Thirty-eight years old,
and still scared of the dark. His mouth quirked with a
humorless smile. Scared not of what the dark might hold,
but of what it didn't. If he pretended hard enough, he could
almost hear her breathing beside him, feel the dip of the
mattress as she shifted in her sleep, murmuring. When
they'd spent their first full night together and he'd wak-
ened to hear her talking in her sleep, he'd thought she was
dreaming of another man. But then he'd listened closely and
realized she was arguing with herself, muttering about slow
viruses and nucleic acids and prions and things he'd never
comprehend if he lived forever. She hadn't remembered any
of it in the morning, and he used to tease her about demanding extra pay for all the work she did in her sleep.

Ah, Jill, he thought wearily, where did we go wrong? Why
did you stop trusting me, closing me out of your life when
you needed me the most? What are you hiding?

He opened his eyes and sat up with a heavy sigh, turning on the lamp and looking at his watch. Eight-thirty. He was supposed to be there by nine. He rubbed his stubbled cheek noisily and yawned, then stood up and stumbled sleepily into the bathroom and turned on the shower. At least he'd slept. He'd come back to his rental condo after leaving Jill and had collapsed across the bed without bothering to do more than kick off his sand-filled shoes. And, for the first time in weeks, he'd fallen into a deep and dreamless sleep that had lasted for hours.

He looked at his own reflection in the foggy mirror above the sink, trying not to wince. Deep lines bracketed his mouth, finer ones his eyes. Those eyes, slate-gray, were troubled and thoughtful at the moment. "That's what you get for breaking the rules, my friend," he reminded himself. "You weren't supposed to fall in love with her. That was never in the game plan."

The lithe redhead talking to Brett leaned across to take a canapé from a passing plate, and managed to press her breasts against his arm. Nancy Whelan gave a snort and rammed her elbow into Jill's ribs. "I told you she'd latch onto him within five minutes," she murmured. "How about a small wager on how long before they leave? I say twenty minutes, tops."

Jill laughed and bit into a smoked oyster. "You're incorrigible, Nan! I think the only reason you have these parties is to see whose marriage you can break up. Isn't she a senator's wife or something?"

"Or *something*." Nancy's eyebrow soared. "He's left his wife for her, I hear, but there's been no word yet on a divorce. I doubt there'll be one. She'll take him for everything he's got—the wife, I mean—and even he's not stupid enough to risk a scandal this close to elections."

"I'm surprised you didn't invite him. *And* his wife." Jill gave her hostess an amused look. It was impossible to tell how old Nancy Whelan was. She had that kind of flamboyant, reckless beauty that was ageless, although if she really had done some of the things she said she'd done, she had to be nearer seventy than the fifty she claimed.

"Hardly," Nancy drawled. "He's a boor, and she's a bore. They're a perfect match, but are hardly the sort one would invite to a party unless under political duress." She gave Jill a conspiratorial smile. "Besides, darling, I enjoy excitement and scandal, not murder. It's so banal."

"Speaking of scandal," Jill asked with amused bluntness, "is that why you invite me to these things?"

Nancy's eyes widened. "Of course, darling! I mean, you do have a cachet of... shall we say, illicit excitement. Every woman needs a whiff of scandal linked to her name now and again. It drives men mad." She put her arm around Jill's shoulders and hugged her. "When your aunt told me she was lending you her condo for as long as you wanted it, I was ecstatic!" She waved a well manicured and elegantly bejeweled hand in an indolent gesture that took in the entire room. "I needed new blood, darling. Everyone here knows each other's secrets by now, and my little parties were becoming humdrum."

"What lies are you telling this delectable creature now, Nan?" Nancy's young husband strolled to join them, champagne glass in hand. He smiled at Jill, but he had eyes only for Nancy, the adoration in them unfeigned.

As always, Jill felt a fleeting pang of jealousy. Nancy and Richard had been married for nearly fifteen years and were still as avidly in love now as they'd ever been, the age difference of two decades seeming to enhance whatever magic held them together. How could they have been so certain, she found herself wondering as she watched them trade the silly small talk of longtime lovers.

Love wasn't something you could isolate from a cell and study. You couldn't prepare a slide of love and peer at it through an electron microscope. But how, if you couldn't see it and study it and unlock its secrets, could you possibly know it when you found it? If you couldn't run tests to see how it reacted in all varieties of situations and stresses, how could you possibly know it would survive?

She gave her head a shake, bewildered by the complexities of a world she didn't really understand. She'd spent so many years engrossed in cellular chemistry, taking things down to their most basic states, that she sometimes wondered if she'd lost touch with this other reality. DNA didn't hold half the mystery of one of Nancy's parties!

"There." Nancy gave her another nudge in the ribs. "What did I tell you? He's got his hand on her—"

"We're nearly out of hors d'oeuvres, Nan."

"Tell the caterer, darling," Nancy murmured, her eyes never leaving Brett and the redhead. "Ten minutes, Jill. He's going glassy-eyed." She looked at Jill suddenly, eyes shrewd. "You don't mind, do you? I mean, you did come with him. And he is a purely delectable hunk of man. If you like, I can send Richard over to distract her."

"Don't be silly, Nan. I'm enjoying this as much as you are." Jill gave Nancy a dry smile. "I brought Brett tonight because you hate it when I turn up without a man. Besides, I know you find him interesting."

"Interesting is an understatement," Nancy purred. "He's got a build like Apollo, and a face like mortal sin itself. For the first time in years, I find myself contemplating breaking at least one of the Commandments."

"Only one?" Jill laughed. "You're slowing down, Nancy."

"Hmm." Those sharp blue eyes fastened onto Jill again. "Are you sleeping with him yet?"

"Nan!"

"Thought not. You really ought to consider it, darling. He looks as though he's got all the necessary equipment— and knows how to use it, too."

"Nancy!"

"Yes, yes, I know we've discussed this before." Nancy dismissed Jill's protest with a wave of her hand. "But you're not getting any younger, darling. Celibacy's admirable when one's in mourning, but it's certainly not something that should be carried to extremes." Her eyes glowed. "I've taken steps to remedy that, I should warn you. In fact, he should be here soon. I told him nine."

"Him?" Jill looked at Nancy sharply. "What are you up to?"

"Nothing." Nancy looked spectacularly innocent. "I simply invited a very interesting man to join us, that's all."

"Nancy, there's never any 'that's all' with you. You're up to something. Now tell me, or I'll go over there and pry that redheaded limpet off Brett and go home with *him*."

"Promise you'll take him to bed, and I'll let you off the hook," Nancy said with a salacious smile. "But now, it's too late. He just came in."

"Who came in?" Jill wheeled around to look at the door. The spacious living room was filled with a kaleidoscope of milling, chatting people, some of whom Jill knew, many she didn't. The lighting was deliberately low so the room was bathed in a soft golden glow that made eyes and diamonds sparkle, and the hum of voices had grown to a quiet roar over the past hour. But as far as Jill could tell, there was no one there who hadn't been there all evening.

"You're almost late, you handsome devil," Nan said suddenly. "Good, I see you got yourself a drink. Now come over here, because there's someone I want you to meet. Jill, darling, do stop staring at that door as though you expected Satan himself to step through it.''

Jill turned. ''Nancy, I didn't see who you—'' She stopped dead, finding herself staring at the open throat of a man's shirt instead of into Nancy Whelan's bright-blue eyes. She blinked, then looked up, drawing in her breath sharply.

''Hello, Jill.''

Her voice dropped to a whisper in shock. ''How did you get in here?''

''I believe you know Hunter Kincaide, don't you, Jill?'' Nancy slipped her arm through Jill's as though to prevent a panicked escape. ''When I heard Hunt was in town, I thought it would be nice to include him.'' Nancy smiled at Jill, her eyes snapping with mischief, then she looked up at Hunter appraisingly. ''You're getting better looking every time I see you, Hunt. A little grayer on top than I remember, maybe, but still enough to turn a woman's head.''

''And you're as beautiful—and as deadly—as *I* remember, Nan.'' Hunter lifted his champagne glass in a toast. ''Thanks.''

''Anytime.'' She gave him a sly wink, then patted Jill's arm. ''I'm putting him in your care, darling. Do be good to him, all right? Mature unattached males who are neither painfully unattractive nor dangerously antisocial are as rare as gemstones.''

''Nancy!'' But Nancy was already disappearing into the crowd and Jill's cry of desperation was lost in the roar of laughter and voices. She turned to glare up at Hunter. ''This was a setup,'' she hissed. ''You put her up to this! What did you have to promise her to pull this off?''

''An invitation to the White House next time she's in Washington.'' Hunter gave her a slashing smile. ''It'll mean calling in most of my markers, but I figure it was worth it.''

"For two cents I'd walk out of here right now," Jill said in a low, angry voice. "It would serve both of you right. But I'm damned if I'll give everyone in this room the satisfaction of seeing the infamous Jill Benedict back down from a confrontation with the equally infamous Hunter Kincaide."

"Flattering both of us, aren't you?"

"Don't be naive, Hunter. You didn't get invited to this party because of any promise to smuggle Nancy into a White House dinner, or even because you're hot stuff as a writer. You got invited because I was here. And the only reason *I'm* here is because everyone wants to catch a glimpse of Jill Benedict, the woman who falsified test results in the famous Phoenix lab fraud, pretending to have found a cure for MS to keep her research funding from being cut off. That medical scandal story you're working on is bound to get you a Pulitzer, but even that's not as fascinating to these people as the fact that it was you who pulled the rug out from under my feet at Phoenix." She smiled at him coldly. "They're waiting for a fight, Hunter. Want to humor them?"

"No." Hunter's face was set in that hard, intractable expression she'd seen so often before. He reached out and whipped a glass of champagne off a passing tray, then shoved it into her hand. "Drink that."

"Peace offering?" she asked sarcastically. "You're an optimist if you think it's going to be that easy."

"Tranquilizer. I figure with enough of them under your belt you'll be calm enough for us to talk without turning it into a war."

"There isn't enough champagne in all of France to calm me down that much." But she did take a sip of the champagne, feeling the bubbles race to her head. She ran an appraising glance over him, taking in the deceptively casual cut of his pale-yellow linen sports jacket, the cotton shirt, open at the throat, the fashionably baggy white slacks. He was freshly shaven and he'd obviously just washed his hair. It needed a trim, as usual, the top lying carelessly where a fast swipe with his fingers had left it.

No two ways about it, she admitted grudgingly, Nancy was right: There was something about the man that turned heads. He had the kind of rough-and-ready features that improved with age, every added scar and line making him a little more dangerous and compelling. Except for that ridiculous dimple in his left cheek, she found herself thinking. It showed with even the faintest hint of smile, like right now, and gave him an endearingly boyish charm that was irresistible.

The dimple deepened as he watched her watch him. "I haven't changed that much, Boston."

"Too bad." For some reason, she found the acid little shots unsatisfying. They were just words, she realized slowly. Time had stripped them of their emotion. And he was making it too easy, almost as though he were trying to give her an excuse to lash out.

"I've missed you, Jill," Hunter suddenly murmured. "I don't think I realized just how much until I saw you this morning."

"I can't imagine why."

"You know why, Jill."

She glanced up at him, then away just as quickly, confused by a whirlwind of conflicting emotions. She hated him and loved him. Wanted to turn away from him and wanted him to hold her. "Yes," she whispered, remembering. "I suppose I do."

"You've lost weight."

She shrugged, smiling. "A woman can never be too rich or too thin, as the saying goes."

"Your mother said you were pretty down for those first two months—not eating, not sleeping, not talking. She said you just stared out the window, as though you were pulling into yourself to shut out the world. She said that when your aunt offered you this condo she and your father had to practically drag you down here."

"Yes, well, I guess I had a reason to be pretty down for a while." She met his gaze evenly. "I'm okay now, so you didn't need to come and check on me. Mom or Dad come down now and then to make sure I'm eating and sleeping. And talking."

A faint smile brushed Hunter's mouth. "Your mother said you were working and happy down here. She suggested you'd be even happier if I stayed the hell away."

"She was right." Jill lifted her glass to take another sip of champagne when she saw Brett making his way through the crowd toward her. His face was set with determination and she smiled in welcoming relief. "Hi!"

"Hi, yourself. Sorry I got sidetracked."

Jill smiled, sensing more than actually seeing Hunter stiffen. "Yes, I saw her. Pretty."

Brett's face broke into a cheery grin. "Barracuda." He nodded toward her glass. "Get you another one of those?"

Jill nearly smiled again, realizing that Brett was deliberately ignoring a glowering Hunter. Both were practically bristling, and the air was filled with static tension. "I'm fine, Brett, thanks. This is Hunter Kincaide, by the way. Hunter, I'd like you to meet Dr. Brett Douglass."

Hunter lifted his head like a stag scenting the wind, eyes narrowed. She could feel Brett stir restlessly beside her. Then Hunter nodded stiffly, not offering the other man his hand. Brett slipped his arm around Jill's shoulders and smiled coolly, looking very relaxed and comfortable. "So you're the famous Bulldog Kincaide. I've heard a lot about you. I've even read some of your stuff.''

Hunter's eyes narrowed even more at the word ''stuff'' and Jill had to bite her lip to keep from laughing aloud. But he merely smiled, then looked at Jill. ''How about dinner later?''

''I'm not hungry.''

''I'm paying.''

''Not nearly enough.''

''More than you suspect,'' he replied quietly, his eyes serious. ''We have to talk, Jill.''

''Sorry, Kincaide,'' Brett put in with soft menace. ''I'm taking Jill to dinner tonight. If you'll excuse us . . .''

''Brett!'' Jill succumbed to the laughter as Brett firmly steered her across the room. She caught a glimpse of Hunter's face before it disappeared in the crowd and felt a pang of reasonless regret. She ignored it and turned her attention to Brett instead. ''Since when were we going out to dinner tonight?''

''Since your old nemesis turned up,'' Brett said with a growl. ''Do you want me to get rid of him?''

Jill was tempted to say yes, but knew she was lying even as she thought it. ''No,'' she sighed, daring a quick glance around the room. Hunter was nowhere to be seen and she wondered if he'd left, her heart giving a painful thump at the possibility. Damn it, she thought irritably, what was the matter with her? Hunter Kincaide had used her in the ugliest way possible, seducing her both physically and emotionally to gain her trust, then betraying that trust to get his story. Her heart still ached with the bruises he'd left on it.

''He's got a hell of a lot of nerve, turning up after what he did to you,'' Brett muttered. ''Are you going to be okay? If you want to go home—''

"I live next door, Brett," Jill reminded him dryly. "I'm sure I can make it on my own." She looked at him and found him staring interestedly across the room. Following his gaze, she saw a tall, shapely blond woman talking with Nancy and Richard. She smiled. "Go get 'em, cowboy."

He grinned sheepishly. "Sure you'll be all right by yourself? It doesn't seem right, coming here with you then just leaving you on your own all night."

"I dragged you to this affair because I thought you'd enjoy meeting some of Nan's friends, not because I expected you to glue yourself to my side all evening, Brett. Now stop worrying about me and go over there and introduce yourself to that ravishing blonde before someone else does."

Brett gave her a wolfish grin and a swift kiss on the forehead. "You're one in a million, sweetheart." Then his face turned serious. "If Kincaide gives you any trouble, I want you to let me know. And I don't mean just here. If he starts bothering you at your apartment, no matter what the time, phone me—"

"—and you'll be over in ten minutes, trailing speeding tickets like confetti," Jill said with a laugh. "I'll be fine, Brett. Believe me."

He gave a grunt that clearly indicated what he thought of the entire situation, but he didn't argue. He kissed her again, then started threading his way through the crowded room toward the blonde, looking very much like a barracuda himself. Jill looked around, didn't see anyone she felt like talking with and wandered toward the wall of glass overlooking the beach. A young waiter with an incandescent smile spun a tray in front of her and she took another glass of champagne. She sipped it absently, staring down at the gardens and pool.

Floodlights turned it into a surrealist landscape of palmettos and cacti at night, tall coconut palms casting shadows over everything. Reflections from the underwater pool lights danced across the windows of the surrounding apartments like emerald fireflies, and in the distance, beyond the velvet of the well tended lawn and the broad sweep of meticulously raked sand, starlight glittered off restless, untamed waves. Five more minutes, she decided, then she'd thank Nancy and go home.

"Like a walk on the beach?"

Jill stiffened. He'd come up behind her so stealthily she hadn't known he was there until he'd spoken. His breath stirred her hair slightly and she could feel his warmth, smell the clean, masculine scent of him, uncluttered by cologne or aftershave. Or the familiar fog of cigarette smoke, she suddenly realized with amusement. Had he quit again? He'd quit four times in the three weeks they'd known one another in North Carolina. Three weeks. It didn't seem possible she could have fallen so hopelessly in love in three meager weeks.

Hunter strolled past her, hands in pockets, and stared out the window with her. "What are you thinking about?" he asked after a moment.

Jill's mouth curved in an involuntary smile. "I was thinking about turtles. Baby sea turtles, as a matter of fact." She nodded toward the brilliantly lit sand and the dark, spangled water. "When baby sea turtles hatch at night, they head for bright lights—instinct tells them that it's moonlight on the sea. But the beaches up and down Florida's coasts are wall-to-wall buildings. The hatchlings get confused and can't tell which way to go. Sometimes they wander in circles until they die of exhaustion. In some places, the streets along the beaches are covered with little squashed turtles that have wandered out into traffic to follow a streetlight to the sea."

"Can't the conservation people do something?"

'They're trying, but most people come down here and get their tans and play their golf and never think about something as simple as lights and sea turtles. And most of the condominiums and hotels don't care. Let's face it—multimillion dollar corporations have more on their minds than baby turtles. If you want a story, Kincaide, write that one.'' She turned to look up at him. ''But you're not interested in writing stories about victims of injustice, are you? You prefer creating your own.''

He was still staring out the window as though fascinated by something there in the dark. ''We can't go on like this, Jill.''

''No.'' She sighed, looking at that strong, uncompromising profile. ''Maybe it is a good thing you came down here. We never really said goodbye during all the shouting. Maybe we need to put a proper end to it once and for all.''

Again, it didn't give her as much satisfaction as it should have to see him wince. He drew in a deep breath as though to say something, then eased it out between his gritted teeth instead. A long moment later, he turned and leaned his shoulder against the window frame, looking at her, his expression carefully noncommittal. ''That hunk you came with someone special?''

''A friend.''

''Pretty protective for just a friend.''

''Maybe he thinks I need protecting.''

''You don't need protecting from me, Jill,'' he said quietly, his eyes holding hers.

''No?'' She raised a skeptical eyebrow. ''Seems to me I could have used some protection in Chapel Hill.''

''You knew what you were doing in Chapel Hill. You came into my bed of your own free will, eyes open.''

''Did I?'' she challenged, knowing it was true but hating to admit it. It was hard to believe she'd ever been that gullible! "You're a real sweet-talker when you put your mind to it, Kincaide."

Hunter ignored the barb. "And Douglass? What kind of a sweet-talker is he?"

"He tries."

"And?"

Jill looked at him in disbelief, then laughed and shook her head. "Brett Douglass and I aren't sleeping together, if that's what you're asking in your uniquely tactful way."

"I've been thinking about that a lot, Jill." His gaze caught hers. "Remembering what it felt like to—"

"You want to watch that," Jill put in swiftly. "Thinking's never been your strong suit, Kincaide. You run on instinct, not reason. You told me that yourself, remember?"

"Do you remember what we were doing when I told you?" he asked in a purring voice, eyes holding hers boldly.

"No." Jill gave a dismissive toss of her head and turned away, a hot blush transfusing her cheeks as every vivid, erotic detail of that discussion came back. They'd been making love when Hunter had growled, "Stop analyzing what's happening, Jill, and just let it happen. Turn off that beautiful mind and let your body take over. Let it feel what I'm doing, sweetheart. Let it tell you what you want, what you need...." And it had, she recalled with heartstopping clarity. For the first time in her life she knew the real meaning of passion, and the magic he'd shown her that night had left her breathless with wonder. And love.

A faint smile played around his mouth as though he knew exactly what she was thinking. "So tell me about the good Doctor Brett. What's he a doctor of? Broken hearts?"

"Jealous?"

"Yes."

He said it so matter-of-factly that it caught Jill by surprise. She stared at him, seeing the unfeigned pain in his

eyes, suddenly realizing that perhaps Hunter hadn't come
through this nightmare as unscathed as she'd thought.
"Brett's the local veterinarian," she said quietly. "I've been
helping him with his work with RAVEN."

"RAVEN?" Hunter's brows met. "Sounds like a terror-
ist organization." He grinned suddenly, his eyes and
expression gentling. "Or government. You haven't gone and
got yourself mixed up with the CIA or something, have
you?"

"No!" Jill tried not to laugh, but found it impossible not
to. "It stands for Residents Assisting Victims of Environmental Negligence." Hunter's eyebrows rose to impressive
heights and Jill's smile turned into an outright grin, enjoying watching him try to fit something called RAVEN into the
life of the woman he'd once thought he knew.

"Brett started RAVEN here on Sanibel three years ago to
educate people about the environmental damage local de-
velopers and industry are doing to the Florida wetlands re-
gions. The group holds beach walks and birding trips, gives
lectures at schools, collects alligators that have strayed into
residential areas, nurses hurt animals, that sort of thing. We
work hand in hand with a group called CROW—Care and
Rehabilitation of Wildlife—who do a terrific job taking care
of injured and orphaned animals."

"Crows and ravens…" He shook his head, looking at her
quizzically. "That's what you're doing now? Playing wet
nurse to stray alligators?"

"Occasionally." The expression on Hunter's face made
Jill laugh. "If you want to get technical, I've been studying
the cellular and DNA changes in wetlands wildlife caused by
ingestion of pesticides and toxic waste." He couldn't quite
hide his surprise, and Jill smiled dryly. "I'm as welcome in
most labs these days as an outbreak of anthrax, but there are

still one or two willing to risk having me on the premises. RAVEN jumped at the chance, Ethics hearings or not.''

Hunter smiled. ''Hardly surprising. It's not every day a bunch of hometown conservationists can hire their own biochemist, especially one of your caliber. They'd be glad to have you if you wore leper bells.''

Jill managed a weary smile. ''As far as most people are concerned, I do. I still have friends here and there who'll talk to me in public, but most look the other way if they see me coming. Admitting you know Jill Benedict these days isn't healthy for one's career, especially if you're bucking for tenure or your funding's up for renewal.'' She gave up on the smile, surprised at how strong the hurt still was. ''I can't say I blame them; I'd probably do the same thing in their shoes. Even the ones who think I was innocent can't take the chance.''

She looked up angrily, eyes suddenly stinging. ''I used to think medical research was an honorable profession, full of people dedicated to helping mankind. Instead, I found it's just as cutthroat and manipulative as any Fortune 500 business, full of little tin gods who'll do anything or hurt anyone to save their precious grants or work their way up another rung on the tenure ladder. I'm glad I'm out of it, you know that? It's all a lie.''

Hunter held her angry stare calmly, then reached out and brushed something from her cheek. His fingertips came away wet. ''Sooner or later you had to have some of that starry-eyed idealism knocked out of you, Jill. You've been lucky that it's taken this long. You spent so much time studying your miniature worlds that sometimes you forget to take a good look at the real one around you. We're all just human beings; none of us are saints.''

''But *they're* supposed to be, damn it!'' Jill heard the childish anger in her voice and stopped. She managed an unsteady laugh. "You always told me I was a Pollyanna. I guess you knew what you were talking about after all."

"You always told me I was a hard-nosed cynic with an outlook on life that made vinegar sweet." He grinned, his cheek dimpling. "We were good for each other, Jill. Just like one of your chemical reactions."

"Oil and water, maybe."

"Or nitro and glycerin."

"You'd make a lousy chemist, Kincaide." But Jill found herself laughing, her resolve melting under that damnable playfulness she'd once found so irresistible. He'd always been able to touch something inside her that yearned to laugh and be silly, and of all the things she missed about those three magic weeks in Chapel Hill, that was the most poignant.

"I might not be a chemist," he drawled, "but I know good chemistry when I see it."

"You think that's what we had?" she asked flippantly.

"Have," he purred, eyes gleaming in the light reflected from the pool. "What we still have, Jill."

"No." She said it very firmly, but his warm liquid gaze held hers, filled with memories, and a little shiver wound its way languorously through her. Oh, no, she thought despairingly. Not again! I thought I was over him once and for all. Realizing, even as she was thinking it, that she was far from being over Hunter Kincaide.

"Let's get out of here," he said suddenly, his voice rough-timbred. He drew her to him and started moving through the crowd, body half-curved around hers as though protecting her.

Jill knew she should be protesting, that if she let Hunter ease her out of the safety of Nancy's party she was lost. But instead she simply followed as he headed toward the door.

Four

Hunter wove her through the crowded room with the skill of a small-town politician collecting votes, smiling and murmuring farewells here and there but never slowing enough to be trapped by a would-be conversationalist. Nancy put up a flurry of protest near the door, but found herself chatting to thin air as Hunter pushed Jill into the corridor and pulled the door closed.

He sucked in a huge lungful of cool, clean air as they walked down the corridor. "That's better. I nearly hyperventilated trying to breathe in all that secondhand cigarette smoke."

"Don't tell me you're quitting again."

"A couple of months ago." He stopped in front of a pale-blue door, one down from Whelan's. "Give me your key."

"I . . ." She hesitated, then sighed and did as he asked.

Hunter unlocked the door and pushed it open. A puff of sweet-scented air met him, laden with Jill's subtle perfume, and something twisted inside him so hard it hurt. Her apartment in Chapel Hill had smelled the same way, filled with the scent and feel of her even when she wasn't there. He'd wait for her there sometimes, stretched out on her sofa, pretending she was beside him. And after she'd left, before the movers had cleaned everything out, he'd spent two nights there, tossing and turning in the bed they'd shared, the sheets so filled with her that with his eyes closed it was as though she'd never left at all. Only his arms betrayed him, reaching out for the silken warmth that wasn't there.

Jill stepped through the door and paused, glancing up at him, clearly uncertain about what to do next. Had she slammed the door in his face he'd have retreated gracefully, but she hesitated a moment too long and Hunter, used to taking advantage of hesitation and open doors, slipped through before she remembered she didn't want him there.

The foyer was dark and still, lit only by light playing across the ceiling where an open doorway led to the living room. Reflections dancing off the pool in the courtyard, Hunter realized, looking around for a light switch. Jill was fumbling for it, too, and as their hands brushed Hunter distinctly heard Jill's indrawn breath. He looked down to find her staring up at him, her eyes wide and a little frightened.

"Jill." He just whispered it, hearing his voice catch on the word, and in the next instant she was in his arms.

"Hold me!" It was just a sobbed cry of anguish as she locked her arms around him. "Oh, Hunter, please hold me!"

He hugged her against him with the fierce desperation of a drowning man. So long, he found himself thinking. God, it had been so long since she'd filled his arms with that feminine warmth he craved so much. Needed. "I've missed you so much. I never knew it was possible to miss someone that much."

"I didn't think you'd bother looking for me," she sobbed. "I didn't think I'd ever see you again."

"I've spent months trying to find you. Trying to convince your parents and friends to tell me where you'd gone." He tightened his arms. "They said you didn't want to see me."

"I didn't." She was sobbing against his chest, each convulsive breath torn from the deepest part of her. "I never wanted to see you again. I hated you so much!"

"I know, sweetheart."

"Just hold me tight."

"I've been going out of my mind, wanting to hold you like this all day," he groaned, burying his face in her hair. "Don't run away from me again, Jill. Promise you won't run away again."

"Oh, Hunter." Her mouth was under his, opening hungrily, and he plundered its ripeness with a groan, drowning in her, wanting more. Her dress dipped almost to the waist in back and he ran his hands over the bared skin greedily, his already precarious self-control nearly snapping as she moved urgently against him, breasts and taut stomach and long, slender thighs fitting to the male contours of him with mind-spinning familiarity.

He wrenched his mouth from hers and buried his face against her neck. "All I've been able to think about is what you've been going through, treated like an outcast, seeing your picture plastered over every two-bit periodical in the country. If I'd known this was going to happen, I'd have—" *Would have what?* he asked himself despairingly. She'd been right this morning when she'd said he'd do it all again. He didn't know any other way. "Oh, hell, Jill, I never wanted any of this to happen."

"I know." She said it in a small, wet voice, swallowing a sob halfway through. Sniffing, she pulled back, groping for her handbag.

"Here." Hunter pulled a wad of tidily folded tissues from his jacket pocket, peeled one off and handed it to her.

Jill laughed damply and blew her nose. "You're the only man I ever knew who takes the Boy Scout creed of always being prepared seriously."

Hunter smiled, handing her another one to wipe her eyes. "Self-defense. Sooner or later every reporter worth his oats winds up with a distraught woman crying on his shoulder." Or a child, he added silently, thinking of Managua and Belfast and a hundred other horror-filled places.

"I never thought of myself as being the distraught type," Jill said with a tiny smile, wiping her cheeks dry. "I'm sorry. I didn't know I was going to do that. In my fantasies, I was always Ingrid Bergman, very cool and unemotional as I told you calmly to go to hell."

"And who was I? In these fantasies?"

"A cross between Errol Flynn and the Boston Strangler."

"Ouch."

Jill looked up at him. "I hated you, Hunter. More than I ever thought possible."

"And now?"

"Now?" She shook her head slowly, her eyes never leaving his. "I don't know. When I saw you on the beach this morning it all came flooding back, the anger and hurt, the hate. But I just feel empty now." She shrugged, smiling faintly. "You always told me I should get in touch with my feelings, that you'd like to see something get to me."

"I'm just sorry I had to be the one to do it," Hunter said softly, his heart aching for the pain he'd caused her.

"No more apologies. Would you like a cup of coffee?"

Hunter looked at her sharply. Was this a peace offering, or was she just being polite? She could call up that very proper Bostonian upbringing of hers to chilling effect when she chose to, and she knew it drove him crazy when she hid her emotions behind that barricade of impeccable good manners. But she was looking at him almost shyly, and he found himself remembering how nervous and endearingly awkward she'd been that first night they'd spent together. "Sure. Thanks."

She nodded, then walked toward what Hunter supposed was the kitchen. Alone, he gazed around at the luxurious furnishings curiously, then strolled into the living room. Carpeted in ice-blue and mirrored on two sides, the room's furnishings were expensive and cold, dotted in precisely angled groups. There were the correct number of color-coordinated prints on the walls and the requisite two or three art books sitting on the glass coffee tables. The overall effect was intimidatingly aloof, and Hunter found himself thinking of the friendly clutter in Jill's apartment in Chapel Hill, with its wall-to-wall books and overstuffed furniture.

"Do you still take it black, with a half pound of sugar?" Jill walked across to a coffee table and set down a tray.

Hunter grinned. "I've cut it down to one spoon."

"Still bad for you," she replied disapprovingly. "You can sit down, you know."

"I was afraid to."

Jill looked startled, then she laughed, wrinkling her nose as she looked around the room. "It's awful, isn't it? Aunt Steph paid a fortune to have it done, but to my mind it's like living inside an iceberg."

Hunter scooped up a generous spoonful of sugar from the bowl, glanced at Jill, then sighed and put half of it back. He put what was left in one of the mugs of steaming coffee and stirred it. "Nice of them to let you use it."

"Uncle Roland insisted they buy it as a retirement home, in spite of the fact he's still Chief Surgeon at Boston General with no plans for retirement in sight. Aunt Steph's too busy with charity work and the Symphony to come down by herself. They've spent maybe four weeks here in the last year and a half, and they like someone to be here to keep an eye on it."

"Beats Boston this time of year."

"True." There was an awkward silence, and Hunter knew she was thinking the same thing he was: that if it hadn't been for him she'd have been spending November in Chapel Hill, not Boston, and that she wasn't on Sanibel by choice but because she had nowhere else to go.

He sat on the edge of a white brocade chair and stirred his coffee, wondering how or where to start. He'd rehearsed it so often he thought he knew all the words by rote, but now he was here and all the tidy phrases sounded trite and overblown. It was like threading his way through jungle, he thought gloomily. The shadows were fraught with traps and dead ends, and one misstep could leave him floundering around in quicksand, sinking fast.

Jill stood by the window, watching Hunter. He was stirring his coffee, staring absently into the cup as though hoping to find life's answers, and she wondered what he was thinking about. He'd changed since Chapel Hill. He was more introspective now, more...gentle. She smiled. Gentle was not a word she'd ordinarily use to describe the man sitting in front of her. Not that he wasn't capable of great gentleness at times, she mused, thinking of their lovemaking. But even then she'd always sensed tension simmering just under the surface, held tightly in control. He'd always seemed on the verge of exploding with sheer energy, especially when working on a story, but now all that seemed burned out of him. She thought of Chapel Hill, of the man he'd been then, and found herself wondering what had happened during the last seven months to change him.

She had happened, Jill reminded herself. Was it possible that she hadn't been the only one who'd been hurting over those seven long months? She frowned. She'd changed; why not Hunter? If she'd lost some of her wide-eyed idealism, if the Phoenix affair had left her disenchanted and a little bitter, she'd also come through it with a clearer understanding of personal strengths she'd never suspected before, of what was important to her and what wasn't. Could the same thing have happened to Hunter?

Impulsively, she walked across to where he was sitting. A tangle of sandy-brown hair had fallen across his forehead and she ran her fingers through it, brushing it back. Hunter glanced up at her, then smiled and took her hand in his. He started kissing her inner wrist. The feather touch of his lips was so gently coaxing it made her tingle, and she sighed deeply and sat on the arm of the chair beside him, slipping her arm around his neck and resting her cheek on the top of his head.

"Things sure are a mess, aren't they?" she murmured half to herself. She stroked his hair back from his temple with her fingertips, breathing in the clean scent of his shampoo.

"We caused each other a lot of grief," he agreed quietly. He set his cup aside and leaned back in the chair, resting his head on the cushioned back and gazing up at her with a half smile. "You've been haunting me for these past seven months, lady. Now and then I'd catch a whiff of your perfume and nearly break my neck trying to find you in the crowd. I'd wake up in the night swearing I could feel you beside me, but when I reached out there'd be no one there. The other evening one of the local TV stations replayed a tape of an interview you'd done. I looked up and saw you on the screen and it felt as though I'd been kicked by a horse." He traced the bowed outline of her mouth with his fingertip. "I've missed you."

Jill smiled and caught his finger between her teeth, biting it lightly. "I miss you some days," she admitted finally. She ran her finger along his lower lip and he opened his mouth, touched her finger with the tip of his tongue. A tingling shiver ran through her, settling in her pelvis with an erotic precision that was impossible to ignore; she found herself lowering her mouth to his.

His lips were softly inviting and they coaxed hers apart effortlessly, opening her to the gentle probe of his tongue. The taste of him was so familiar and achingly perfect that she sighed with pleasure as he explored the recesses of her mouth with lazy contentment, one hand cupping her head, the other settling on her bare thigh just below the hem of her dress. His kiss deepened and, feeling her respond, he slid his hand slowly up her thigh until his thumb just brushed the soft mound outlined with erotic explicitness by her thin cotton panties.

She started badly, her breath catching, and Hunter laughed softly and removed his hand. "Sorry—habit. And too much wishful thinking."

Don't stop! she wanted to whisper urgently, craving his touch more than she could have thought possible. But something stopped her. A sudden shyness, perhaps. Or maybe just an unwillingness to admit so much vulnerability so soon.

As though sensing her uncertainty, Hunter drew back. Jill sat up unsteadily and brushed her hair off her hot cheeks, wishing her heart would stop its frantic pace. *You're making it too easy for him,* she told herself disgustedly. *This morning you never wanted to see him again and here you are caving in like wet cardboard. You have all the backbone of an amoeba.*

"Going too fast?" Hunter murmured. "I don't want to push you, Jill. I know you need time to get used to having me in your life again. Things ended badly in Chapel Hill, and we've got a lot to resolve, but I just want you to give it a chance."

Is that what she wanted? Jill looked down into those calm gray eyes thoughtfully, toying with a lock of his hair. "I loved you."

"I know." His voice was rough, and the pain in his eyes was unfeigned.

"I swore I'd kill you if I ever saw you again."

A smile flirted around Hunter's mouth and he put his hand to his jaw, rubbing it. "You came close. A couple of my back fillings are still rattling."

Jill had to smile. "I've always been a pacifist by nature, but that felt incredibly good."

"If it'll help, you can do it again."

She shook her head, still smiling, and traced the angle of his rock-solid jaw with a fingertip. "Once was therapy. Twice would be self-indulgence."

Hunter laughed softly, catching her hand in his and kissing her palm. "Is that an offer of amnesty?"

She gazed down at him for a long moment, frowning. Hunter sat quietly under her scrutiny, as though putting himself and their future trustingly in her hands. It was her decision, he seemed to be saying. "I thought I hated you, Hunter. I spent seven months nursing that hate, feeling lied to and betrayed. I thought I never wanted to see you again. But now . . ." She shrugged, the confusion and anger seeming to dissolve and swirl away, tenuous as fog, even as she struggled to put it into words.

Hunter relaxed almost imperceptibly, as though he'd been holding his breath. He reached up and cupped her head in one large hand, tugging her face down to his. "Let's just start all over again, Jill,'' he breathed, moving his mouth on hers. ''You're the most important thing that's ever happened to me.''

Important enough for you to forget about Phoenix? Jill almost asked aloud. She swallowed the words, suddenly not wanting to hear the answer, and kissed him, his freshly shaven skin deliciously smooth. ''I've been following that series of articles on medical fraud you've been working on all summer. It's very good. In fact, it's probably your best work since that Central America piece two years ago. Word's out this one's Pulitzer material, too.''

Hunter drew back, looking at her in surprise. ''You like it? I mean, considering the Phoenix Research story started it, I figured...''

He left the rest unsaid, and Jill smiled. ''You're a good writer, Hunt. Besides, things need shaking out. The medical field's goals have gotten confused, and professional ethics have gone out the window in the rush for publication, for tenure, for funding. The pressure to publish is so great that papers get sent out like confetti, and quantity is put before quality. There have been too many instances of false authorship, fudged data and plagiarism.

''Every lab in the country's fighting for their share of the funding pie, and results are demanded from researchers even if they haven't anything to show. Then there's the ego thing. Natural competition has turned into life-and-death battles, and teamwork is a lost art. Everyone's off in his own little corner, hoarding research, terrified someone is going to beat him into print. It's so easy to distort research results without actually lying, that's the problem. Any reasonably competent researcher can mess around with computerized test data, or even the tests themselves, to verify whatever he wants verified. All it takes is a bit of imagination to turn something run of the mill into the breakthrough of the century."

She caught the expression on Hunter's face, and laughed. "I'm sorry! I jump on that soapbox at the drop of a hat these days. I guess it just hits pretty close to home, after...Phoenix." She frowned, looking away. Even now, the word stuck in her throat like a burr.

"How would you like to help me finish the series?"

Jill looked up, trying not very successfully to smile. "Scientific research fraud from the inside, by the master of fraud herself? Or is that mistress?"

"I'm serious, Jill." He started rubbing the small of her back, his touch warm and soothing. "That series is good, but it could be better. There are a lot of good scientists out there like you who are fed up with what's going on and want to help stop it. But for every one who wants to talk, there are three who don't. There's a lot of funny business going on out there that never gets reported. Private labs sweep it under the rug and 'deal with it' on their own."

"You think they'll talk to me?" She gave a hoot of amusement. "Let Jill Benedict show up in those hallowed halls, Hunter my friend, and you'd think Typhoid Mary herself was loose."

"You still have contacts out there. You can also interpret the information I do get, put it in perspective, give me insights I might miss."

Jill looked at him quizzically. "Do you have any idea what it would do to your series to have my name even remotely associated with it? If you want sensationalism, you'd have it—you'd go off the charts with the kind of headlines that sell at supermarket checkouts. But any hope you have of being taken seriously would go out the window."

Hunter's quicksilver eyes held hers, the pressure of his hand on her back increasing very slightly. "Not after we clear your name, Jill."

Jill stiffened. "Clear my name?"

"You didn't have a damned thing to do with that mess at Phoenix. In fact I'd be willing to bet my life that you were more surprised at what was going on than Dean Ackerton himself."

Jill swallowed, her throat suddenly dry. "The Phoenix story's over, Hunter. I want to forget about it."

"Forget about it?" He frowned. "Jill, you can't just forget about something that important. Those people ruined your life. They cheated and lied to you, to Ackerton, to the public."

Jill pulled away from his hand, looking down at him. "Hunter, I don't want to talk about Phoenix Research."

He stared at her, slate-gray eyes glittering with impatience, and Jill felt something cold run down her back. "Jill, I'm going to blow the story—the real story—wide open, and make those bastards pay for what they did to you. They closed ranks and left you out in the cold, knowing you'd be crucified. I want them for it."

Jill slid off the arm of the chair and hugged herself, suddenly ice-cold. "No."

Hunter stared at her as though not believing what he'd just heard. He leaned forward, elbows on knees, and looked up at her seriously. "Jill, what the hell are you saying? That you don't want the truth to come out?"

"What truth?" She paced restlessly, rubbing her bare arms. "There are a thousand truths, Hunter. A thousand variations on a theme. Leave it alone, all right?"

"A thousand variations on..." He gave an explosive laugh of disbelief. "Jill, truth is truth! There are no shadings, no degrees of truth; it is, or it isn't."

"Oh, you drive me crazy!" She raised her clenched fists in frustration. "You and your black-and-white view of the world! Truth does not have to be absolute, Hunter, when are you going to understand that? We had this same argument in Chapel Hill."

"That's right," Hunter said through clenched teeth, "and I don't want to get into it with you again. I know that in biochemistry, in any field of science, there are gray areas, lots of room for interpretation and theorizing. But I deal with the real world, Jill, not a fairy-tale landscape in a petri dish. Truth has one form: clear and crisp with no fuzzy edges. There is no room for interpretation."

"Oh, you can be so damned arrogant sometimes! Who made you judge and jury, anyway? What gives you the right to force your interpretation of truth on an innocent and gullible public?"

"I don't believe you, Jill. Do you listen to anything you say or do you just wind yourself up and let fly?" Hunter lunged to his feet. "You're talking deliberate cover-up here. You're talking ethics and moral responsibility. You're talk-ing—"

"Stop patronizing me, Kincaide. I don't need a lecture on ethics and moral responsibility from a man who seduces a woman just to get access to her computer codes."

"I did not make love with you to get a look at that damned computer," Hunter bellowed. "If all I'd wanted was system access, there were easier ways of doing it than taking some inexperienced biochemist to bed!"

"I wasn't inexperienced!" Even as she shouted it, Jill realized how ridiculous it was to be more upset over his implied criticism of her lovemaking than his threat to open up the Phoenix story again. Hunter smiled, and she blushed furiously.

"Maybe not technically," he allowed, "but you'll have to admit you were pretty new to the game."

"From your viewpoint, I suppose I was. You may be proud of having slept your way through three dozen countries and as many wars, but I had better things to do with my life than bed every man who crossed my path."

"Jill," he said gently, "that wasn't a criticism. If you want to know the truth, it meant a lot to me when you decided to make love with me. I knew you didn't think of it simply as recreational. It made our lovemaking very special. It made you very special."

She glared at him suspiciously for a moment or two, even though she had to grudgingly admit he probably meant it as a backhanded compliment. Her relative inexperience had caused her an agony of indecision and embarrassment that first night and Hunter, calm and gentle and infinitely patient, had made everything all right.

"I want to know who did it, Jill."

She stared at him in stony silence and Hunter swore under his breath, recognizing that expression all too well. Her usually laughing mouth, lush and deliciously perfect for kissing, was hard and uncooperative. Her firm chin was set at a pugnacious angle, and her eyes, nearly black in the soft lighting, were as intractable as stone. The poisonously polite Bostonian Princess. He swore again, louder this time, and was rewarded by a flash of anger in those coal-black eyes.

"You were set up, lady. You took the fall yourself, and I want to know why. Who really played around with those test results and left you holding the bag? Who are you protecting, Jill? Simon DeRocher? John Conyers? Or maybe Preston Neals himself? I've narrowed it down to those three. Conyers was working most closely with you. DeRocher, as Team Leader, had easiest access to the computer and test samples. And the Director of Labs, Dr. Neals himself, knows something he's not telling.''

Bull's-eye! Hunter nearly smiled. She'd gone pale under the bronze camouflage of her sunburn. "Neals?" he probed gently. "Or were all three of them in on it? I was getting close to it when they closed ranks and Ackerton dumped the entire mess in the lap of the Ethics Committee. A couple more days and I'd have had the whole story."

"Leave it alone, Hunter." Jill's voice was as chilly as her expression. "There is no more story."

"Are you guilty?" He said it challengingly, knowing she'd never be able to lie to him. Even if her mouth said the words, her eyes would give her away.

There was the tiniest hesitation, the hint of bleak despair in her eyes, gone in a heartbeat. "That's up to the Ethics Committee to decide."

"Bull." He couldn't keep the anger out of his voice and he strode across the room and back again, reminding himself that anger had nearly lost her once. "Are they blackmailing you, Jill? Have they threatened you somehow?" Still no reaction. "Damn it, woman, what the—" He caught himself, planting his hands on his hips and staring at the ceiling, mouth compressed, until he had himself under control.

"It's got to be one of five things. You're actually guilty, which I don't believe for a minute. You're doing it for love, which I believe even less. You're doing it for money, which is a faint possibility but not one I can take very seriously. You're still too damned idealistic to be seduced by 'filthy lucre.' That leaves loyalty, and blackmail. If you're taking the blame for this out of loyalty, you're a sucker. And if you're being blackmailed, you need help."

He strode across to stand in front of her, crowding her. But she held her ground, glaring up at him. "Just tell me one thing, Jill," he demanded with quiet intensity. "Look me straight in the eye and tell me you changed that test data. Tell me that you sat at that computer console yourself and changed those numbers." The silence pulled as tight as piano wire. "Tell me, damn it!"

For half an instant, Hunter thought she was actually going to pull it off. If she had, if she'd become an accomplished enough liar to do that, then he'd lost her *and* the story. But at the very last moment, her resolve crumbled. She let her gaze slip from his and Hunter released his breath, not even aware that he'd been holding it. "Jill . . ." He held up his hands but let them drop, not even knowing what he wanted to say to her. "Jill, I can't help you if you keep fighting me like this."

"I don't need your help," she said hoarsely.

"I wish I could believe that." He ached to put his arms around her, not knowing if he wanted to comfort her or himself.

"That's why you came down here, wasn't it?" she whispered. She glanced up at him, her expression one of unutterable hurt. "Not for me. Just for the . . . story."

"Jill . . ." He cursed himself soundly. Damn it, they were right back to where they'd been in Chapel Hill, their angry words filled with accusation and denial, arguing themselves in circles and getting nowhere. He had his mouth open to tell her it wasn't true, then realized it was pointless. She was too tangled up in whatever had happened at Phoenix to see reason, and too confused at having him back in her life again to listen calmly while he explained it. Time, he told himself impatiently. Give her time.

"I'm renting a time-share condo at the Pirate's Galleon. If you want to talk, or if you just want some company, give me a call." He walked past her and across the living room to the foyer, then turned to look at her. "I came down here for two things, Jill. The Phoenix Story. And you. And I'm not going back to Washington without both." Not bothering to wait for a reply, he let himself out, pulling the door closed behind him with a satisfactory bang.

Five

Phoenix. The word was still on Jill's lips when she awoke, heart pounding, hours later.

She sat up and swept her tangled hair back with trembling fingers. Her cheeks were wet, as though she'd been crying. It wouldn't be the first time. Nor the first time she'd been jolted awake by the sound of her own voice crying out in a nightmare.

She shivered in the air-conditioned chill of the bedroom and pulled the sheet up around her shoulders. Glancing at her bedside clock, she sighed. She'd had four hours of sleep this time. Better than most nights when she was lucky to snatch two or three before the bad dreams came. She knew from experience that it was pointless trying to get back to sleep. Sometimes she read or watched talk shows. Sometimes she simply lay in the dark and waited for dawn, trying not to think.

She glanced at the bedside table again. At the telephone this time, at the number scrawled hastily on the pad beside it. He'd come if she called, a knight in less than shining armor who would wrap his arms around her and warm her and keep the nightmares at bay. They could make love like they had at Chapel Hill, laughing long into the night, and maybe, just maybe, she'd even sleep.

He'd know what to do. He'd be able to help her....

Like a sleepwalker, she lifted the receiver and dialed the number, her hand trembling so badly she had to pause halfway through. It rang and rang and she closed her eyes, praying he wasn't there, praying he was. She flinched when the receiver was picked up and she swallowed, her heart racing.

"Whozit?" His rusty baritone was slurred with sleep, and she could see him lying there in bed, hair tousled, cheeks stubbled and rough. He'd have gotten himself all tangled up in the sheet as he'd floundered around trying to find the phone and he'd be kicking it off now, hating anything binding him. He always slept naked, his body radiating warmth and security like a furnace.

"Anybody there?" He sounded annoyed now. Any moment, Jill knew, and he'd toss the receiver back into the cradle with an oath and roll over, falling asleep instantly.

"Jill?"

It was just a husky whisper, reaching out to her, and Jill froze. She closed her eyes, clenching her hand so tightly around the receiver that it ached, and she called out to him silently. One word, that's all it would take. Just one word, and he'd be at her door in five minutes, sweeping her up into the shelter of his arms, then making fierce love to her, their bodies entwined and wet and seeking.

"Do you want me to come over?"

Yes, she cried silently. *Oh, God, yes.*

Without saying anything, she put the receiver back, her throat aching. "Oh, Hunter," she sobbed into the empty darkness, hugging her knees to her chest and rocking gently. "I need you so much!"

Hunter stared at the phone for a long while after he'd hung up. A warm salty breeze washed through the screened door and the sheer curtains drifted like mist. He could hear the castinet clatter of palm fronds and, pervading his senses like the throb of some giant machine, the rhythmic, muted roar of the surf.

He stood up and wandered to the window, standing there naked looking out over the Gulf. The tide was low and he could see the waves breaking way out on the sandbars, their frilled crests so bright in the moonlight it hurt to look at them.

He glanced back at the phone, wanting to call her, knowing he mustn't. It must have taken a superhuman effort for her to have even dialed his number; she'd never forgive him if he went over there now, sensing her vulnerability. He looked east where the beach curved gently. The lights from the Sea's Glory twinkled between palm fronds like beckoning stars. She was so close he could almost feel her presence, yet there was a chasm between them so wide he wondered if it could ever be bridged.

"I need you, Jill," he whispered to the twinkling lights. "You make me whole."

And Phoenix? he found himself wondering. Just how badly did he want that story? Badly enough to forfeit the woman he loved? Because that's exactly the price he might have to pay....

"Just out of curiosity, gorgeous, did you get any sleep last night?" Brett asked it casually, concentrating on his driving as he aimed the pickup truck up Tarpon Bay Road and floored the accelerator.

Jill gave him a sharp look, clinging to the molded hand grip on the door as they rocketed past the speed limit. "What's that supposed to mean?"

"Don't get hostile," Brett told her mildly. They caught up to a line of rental cars puttering along and Brett had to gear down, muttering under his breath. "That wasn't a subtle way of asking if Kincaide spent the night. If I figured it was any of my business, I'd have come out and asked you straight." He looked at her seriously. "You look like hell, Jill. You're not sleeping, are you?"

She shrugged carelessly, staring out the side window. "I had a nightmare, that's all. I couldn't get back to sleep so I sat up and read that horror novel you lent me. Which is probably why I had the nightmare in the first place." She looked at him and smiled reassuringly. "One restless night does not an insomniac make, good Doctor. I'll sleep like the dead tonight."

Brett looked skeptical, and for a moment Jill thought he was going to press her until she admitted she hadn't had a proper night's sleep in months. But to her relief he seemed to think better of it, and turned his attention back to his driving instead. He braked as the convoy of tourists reached the four-way stop beside the shopping mall. As he eased the truck ahead, he glanced at her. "You've been pretty quiet all day. Want to talk about it?"

Jill smiled. "I have to work this out myself, Brett."

"Yeah, I know," he growled as they shot up Tarpon toward the Sanibel-Captiva highway. "But it kills me, having to stand by doing nothing when I know this thing's eating you up inside."

"You're not doing nothing." She put her hand on his arm. "You're here, and that's a lot. The sound I heard most in those first couple of months was that of slamming doors as all my so-called friends left. Just knowing you're here if I need to talk is the best help you can give me.''

Brett laughed softly and lifted her hand to his lips, kissing it with a gallant flourish. "At your command, dear lady. Dragons slain, castles breached and fair maids defended is my motto. Or was that castles defended and fair maidens breached?''

"Speaking of dragons," Jill said through laughter, "how's old Arnold faring back there?''

"Probably hoping we run into an ice-cream truck.''

Still laughing, Jill craned her neck to peer out the rear window into the back of the truck. The alligator glowered back at her, all six feet of him trussed up like a Christmas turkey. "You've destroyed my image of dragons, Arnold,'' she told him. "Alligators are supposed to eat people, not ice cream and marshmallows.''

Brett gave a snort of laughter. "Don't let the tourist board hear you say that. They spend millions of dollars a year convincing people nothing's going to eat them down here.''

In spite of her joking, Jill eyed the big alligator with respect. Even with his jaws taped together, he radiated danger. "Do you think he'll find his way back into town?''

"Probably." Brett braked for a stop sign, then wheeled out onto the San-Cap highway and accelerated. "As long as people keep feeding them, the 'gators will keep coming back. Why spend your time trying to catch fish and egrets in a swamp when you can live on a golf course and eat marshmallows?''

Jill grinned. "When you put it like that, I can see Arnold's point.'' She relaxed back in the seat and gazed out at the dense vegetation bordering both sides of the highway. It was a riot of green; palmettos fighting for growing space with Brazilian Pepper and coconut palms battling strangler figs and vines. They passed a drawn-out convoy of bicycles heading up the paved cycle path running parallel to the highway. It looked like an extended family outing, the children racing each other for the lead, a handful of grim-looking adults straggling along behind.

She and Hunter had borrowed bicycles from one of her colleagues one afternoon and had spent hours exploring the Raleigh area. It had been a perfect spring day, the sky and air as bright and clear as Waterford glass. They'd stopped for lunch at a tiny French restaurant where Hunter, on a whim that still made Jill smile to think of it, ordered frog's legs, forgetting that Jill had spent too many years in college dissecting rooms.

When the waiter had set the serving dish on the table with a flourish and whipped off the lid, Jill had turned green. Contrite but undaunted, Hunter had sent them back to the kitchen and, to the pitying amusement of the waiter and the disgust of the chef, they had dined instead on hamburgers and fries, nearly choking in their efforts not to laugh at the looks of contemptuous outrage sent their way from the other diners.

They'd made love in a grove of trees by a lake that afternoon. Hunter had laughingly reminded her that if she had the courage to eat a hamburger in a fancy French restaurant, she had the courage to indulge in some postprandial lovemaking in the North Caroline woods. And indulge herself she had, she remembered with a rush of heat to her cheeks.

"What time is it?" Brett suddenly asked. "I told Eastman and Mayhew to meet us at four."

It startled Jill out of her daydreaming. "Quarter to. Time you started wearing that watch Kathy bought you."

"Never think of it until I need it, and then it's too late," he replied with a cheerful grin, swinging the truck into the

entrance of the "Ding" Darling National Wildlife Refuge.
He sped by the Visitors' Center and headed straight for the
wildlife drive.

The wide dirt road, covered with a blinding white layer of
crushed coral and shell, shimmered in the heat as it wound
its way out into the great mangrove swamp on the north side
of the island. Huge sheets of water spread to either side,
black as onyx, confettied with thousands of birds. Almost
as numerous as the birds were the birdwatchers, and the
broad road was dotted with cars, some pulled over onto the
grassy shoulders, others barely inching along as the occu-
pants looked for a glimpse of an alligator or an unusual
bird.

The road entered heavy mangrove and Jill gazed into the
impenetrable jungle of interwoven branches and arching
roots with a little shiver. It was like taking a backward step
in time to the very beginnings of man when the world was
steaming, primordial swamp. She always half expected to
see the sinuous head and neck of a brontosaurus lift curiously above the treetops to stare at them. Snowy egrets and
herons stalked the shallow water, oblivious to tourist cameras or the occasional cruising alligator. Beyond them,
where the water widened into shallow bays, roseate spoon-
bills stood motionless like clusters of exotic pink flowers.
Now and again Jill would catch a glimpse of an anhinga
perched on a low branch, the black-and-white keyboard
pattern of its wings clearly visible as it stretched them out to
dry between dives. And above them, vultures and red-
throated hawks circled tirelessly.

They passed the birdwatching tower, then the mangroves
gave way to open water again. As they rounded a corner, Jill
spotted a Fish and Wildlife Service pickup parked on the
shoulder of the road. Brett pulled in behind it and the two
men who had been standing at the water's edge looked

around. They both grinned in greeting and started strolling back to the road.

"Operation Arnold go okay so far?" one of them asked.

Jill nodded, jumping down from the truck and walking around to the back. "We found him at the ninth tee. The greens' keeper says he likes ice-cream cones and marshmallows best, but will eat fried chicken in a pinch."

One of the men groaned. "When will people learn you can't treat alligators like stray puppies? You can't feed a 'gator, then just pat him on the head and tell him to go away."

"Probably the same time that people in Yellowstone learn not to treat the bears like stuffed toys," Brett replied, releasing the tailgate with a bang. "Okay, boys, he's all yours."

The younger of the two winked at Jill. "Want to give us a hand?"

"I need the two I've got, thanks. I doubt Arnold realizes the expression is figurative."

The other man laughed and started pulling on a pair of heavy work gloves. Gently, the two of them eased the big reptile out of the back of Brett's truck, one holding his taped jaws, the other his tail. Arnold didn't seem particularly upset, and Jill wondered how many times he'd been through this. One of the men retrieved a long metal pole with a loop of thick rope on one end and carefully eased the rope around Arnold's snout, pulling it snug. He nodded to Brett, who cautiously removed the heavy tape he'd previously wound around the animal's jaws.

"Okay, Doc, you'd better get clear." He gave his companion a curt nod, and the two of them lifted the alligator and carried him down to the water's edge. The one holding the tail let go first, scrambling out of the way as Arnold scythed his tail angrily, still held firmly by the rope loop around his snout. Using the long pole like a leash, the older man guided the alligator into shallow water, then released the rope with a flick of his wrist and backed away cautiously. Arnold, either reluctant to return to the wilds or simply not realizing he was free, stayed where he was for a moment or two, glaring at his tormentors. Then he spun around and dashed into deeper water with frightening speed, submerging at once. He surfaced a few dozen feet away and they watched as he swam toward the distant mangroves, serrated body and long, powerful tail undulating from side to side, the picture of predatory evil.

"Well, I guess that's the last of the Marshmallow Marauder," said Jill, shading her eyes against the low-angled sun. "Can't say as I'll miss him. Those guys are bad news as far as I'm concerned."

"Speaking of bad news," Brett said with a chuckle. "There's the finder of bad news in person."

Jill glanced in the direction that Brett was pointing. Two cars had pulled up on the other side of Brett's truck. She could see a handful of people standing near the water, a couple of them videotaping Arnold's leisurely retreat. One of the men left the group of onlookers and strolled toward her, hands shoved deeply into the pockets of his white cotton shorts, sandy hair ruffled by the hot breeze coming in off the water. He was wearing aviator sunglasses, a snug-fitting deep-blue T-shirt, a pair of expensive leather loafers and a reckless smile that broadened as he got closer.

"Douglass." Hunter nodded a greeting to the tall veterinarian and extended his hand. "Thought it was you when I drove by. Looks like a dangerous way to make a living."

To Jill's surprise, Brett took the offered hand and shook it. "From what I've read of some of your exploits, Kincaide, handling live 'gators is kid stuff. They're more predictable than rebel governments, and I've never had one try to shoot me.''

Hunter gave an appreciative chuckle. ''Maybe not, but I've never worked on a story where I was in danger of being eaten alive, either.''

''Playing tourist, or writing a story? Didn't think alligators would be up your alley.''

''They have a lot in common, actually,'' Jill put in with deceptive good humor. She stared at Hunter defiantly, daring him to say a thing about that phone call last night. With luck, she told herself hopefully, he'd awakened this morning thinking it had just been a dream. ''They're both thick-skinned, and as cold-blooded as they come.''

Hunter's teeth flashed and he lounged against the side of the truck, shoving the aviator glasses up onto the top of his head. ''You forgot tenacious.''

''Alligators are tenacious. You're just pigheaded.''

''How about dinner tonight?'' His voice was intimate and his eyes held hers, filled with gentle warmth. And in that instant, Jill knew he not only remembered the call, but he knew she was thinking of it, too. It created a sense of warmth between them she didn't want, a secret that excluded the others, like remembered lovemaking.

''I—I'm busy,'' she stammered, cheeks hot. She turned away quickly and walked around to the passenger side of the truck. A large hand caught the door and held it firmly closed and Jill looked up at Brett questioningly.

''I'm not going back to town yet, Jill. You'd better catch a lift with Kincaide.''

''I'll wait.''

''No.'' Brett spoke gently, but with steely firmness. ''Go back with him, Jill. You've got to get it sorted out between you once and for all.''

''Sort it—?'' She stopped, eyes narrowing.

"He gave me a call last night, and we went out for a drink. We talked."

"About?"

"You, mostly."

"I hope you enjoyed yourselves."

"We talked about Phoenix." Brett looked down at her. "I don't pretend to know what went on up there, Jill, but I do know there's a good chance you're letting yourself be thrown to the wolves protecting someone guilty, someone who's just taking advantage of your loyalty."

Jill's stomach twisted itself into a knot, but she managed to hold Brett's gaze without flinching. "I told you what happened at Phoenix."

"You told me what you wanted me to know. There have always been things that didn't fit. Kincaide filled in some of the details, that's all."

"Kincaide doesn't know the details," she said angrily. "He doesn't deal with truth, he deals with speculation."

Brett looked at her for a long, silent while. "No," he said finally. "I don't think it's just speculation. I think you're throwing away your career, your work—everything important to you—in some sort of cover-up I'm not even sure you understand."

"I understand that Kincaide's got you convinced there's still life in a story that's dead and—"

"He's trying to help you, Jill."

"He's not down here to help me. He's down here trying to get a new Phoenix story out of the ashes of the old one. He just wants his damned Pulitzer!"

"That series of articles on medical fraud he's been working on for the last seven months is one of the most important stories of the decade, Jill. Whatever awards he gets for it would be well-deserved."

"Brett, I—"

"Talk with him."

He wasn't going to be budged, Jill realized. He had the same intractable expression on his face that she'd seen on Hunter's all too often, and she swore at him under her breath and stalked over to the lone car still parked by the truck. Men! There must be thousands of them out there with no interest at all in rescuing maidens and here she had two of them polishing up their armor and sharpening lances. Why didn't they go out and slay somebody else's dragons and leave her alone?

She got in the passenger side of the rental car and slammed the door. In the west, the world was taking fire. Billows of late-day cloud were turning apricot and gold, their outer edges rimmed with silver.

Hunter smiled as he walked back to the car a few minutes later. Jill was sitting still as stone in the passenger's side, shoulders rigid. She didn't even look at him when he got in. "Don't be such a hard case," he told her dryly. He started the car and pulled onto the road. Dust hung in the hot air, thick as talcum. "I didn't follow you out here, if that's what you're thinking," he said after the taut silence had drawn on for minutes. The car started to cool down and he flexed his shoulders to loosen the damp T-shirt.

"Why did you talk to Brett last night?" Jill didn't look at him.

"Because I was worried about you. I wanted to know if anyone's been down here bothering you."

"You could have asked me."

"I wanted answers." He glanced at her. "And I wanted to check him out. You two seemed pretty friendly. I just wanted to see if there was more to it than that."

Jill gave him an impatient look. "And?"

"He said the same thing you did. He's tried, and been shot down cold. He says you're in love with someone else."

"He's wrong," she said flatly, lifting her chin.

"Is he?"

There was another silence, longer this time. Hunter looked at her, but she was staring at her hands, rubbing thoughtfully at a smear of ink on her palm. He smiled and put his hand out, saying nothing, and a moment or two later she slipped hers into it. He curled his fingers protectively around hers and rested it on her denimed thigh. "I didn't mean to push you last night," he said quietly. "I'm a reporter, a good one, but sometimes when I get on the trail of a story I get impatient and I push. I'm sorry." He looked at her. "I don't want to lose you over this, Jill. You're too important to me."

She was silent for a long while, stroking the back of his hand. "Important enough for you to drop the Phoenix story?"

She asked it casually, not looking at him, and Hunter's stomach wrapped itself into a hard, cold knot of fear. Fear of losing Jill, of losing the story. Fear of having to give up one to keep the other. "That sounds suspiciously like blackmail," he said softly. She didn't answer, staring steadfastly at their braided fingers. "Are you saying that if I want you, I'm going to have to forget about digging out the truth on the Phoenix story?" Still, she didn't answer. "Jill?"

Finally, almost imperceptibly, she shook her head, lifting her face to meet his eyes. "I don't know what it means," she whispered miserably. "I don't want to lose you, either, Hunt. I realized that last night, after... after you left." She slid her gaze from his again, and Hunter thought of that two-in-the-morning phone call, of the courage it must have taken her to come even that close to asking for help. She stared down at his hand again, absently stroking it, her touch as gentle and loving as a child's.

Hunter gritted his teeth and took a deep, calming breath, fighting down a sudden urge to stop the car and shake some sense into her. Damn it, how could a woman so dedicated to truth balk when it came to something as simple as this?

Hunter drew in another unsteady breath, feeling as though he were walking on eggs. Don't push her, something warned him. She's having doubts, wondering if maybe you're right, if the truth should be told and damn the consequences.

He found himself thinking about what she'd been going through. It wouldn't be easy for her, participating in a cover-up in the profession she loved. Science was more than a career to her; it was an avocation. If she was guilty of anything it was being too idealistic for her own good. That's probably why it had been simple for whoever *was* guilty at Phoenix to go for so long without being discovered. Jill, too trusting for her own good, would find an anomaly in a test result and think it carelessness. Too principled to think of corruption herself, she'd be the last to suspect it in others.

Those days when things had been falling apart around her must have been a waking nightmare for her. She'd had to watch the thing she loved stripped right down to the politics, the financial sleight of hand, the stealing and lying and cheating that overcomes people in a competitive business. She'd watched people she'd admired brought down, and people she'd considered friends turn their backs on her. And she'd watched someone—probably someone she trusted and respected—set her up to take the blame for the entire thing.

Little wonder she didn't trust anyone. And it was this woman, the one who had once loved and trusted him as deeply as she'd loved and trusted Phoenix, who had the key to all he wanted. What price, he found himself asking again. What price was he willing to pay?

"Jill, let's forget about Phoenix Research for a while, okay?" She looked up uncertainly, and he smiled. "How about a temporary truce? I've been playing tourist all day, and I'm hot, tired and hungry. I'll drop you off, go home to shower and change, then pick you up around eight and we can explore some of Sanibel's nightlife."

Jill stared at him, mind spinning. Part of her wanted to say yes, yet another part of her screamed caution. Was it really Hunter's companionship that tempted her, she wondered, or the thought of spending another long evening in that cold, empty apartment? Either way lay danger.

"I can't." She looked away, knowing he'd see the lie. "I have to...I have work to do. I have tons of material to go through and, and...things." The lie was so obvious she blushed, and she kept her face tucked down so her hair partly shielded her.

Hunter may have sighed. He tightened his fingers briefly on hers, then drew his hand away. They drove on for miles, the silence broken only as she gave him directions through a tortuous maze of unmarked roads that avoided the tourist congestion on Periwinkle Way. He pulled into her elegant driveway and stopped in front of the covered walkway leading to her building.

"If you can't sleep tonight," he said quietly as she slipped out of the car, "call me. We'll go for a walk or something."

Jill looked at him, then away again quickly, nodding.

"I'll be there when you need me, Jill. Just remember that, all right?"

Then he was gone, his late model rental purring softly through the deepening dusk. Jill watched it until the taillights turned off onto the main road, and she took a deep breath of sea-damp air. The resident colony of crows had settled in the sprawling banyan tree in the front garden and were bickering noisily, looking very pedestrian and unexotic amid the tropical foliage. They screamed at Jill as she strolled across the lawn and garden. Small lizards darted this way and that, gray and brown and emerald green, and she wondered how it was possible to feel so desperately unhappy in paradise.

The apartment was silent and still. Jill wandered aimlessly from room to empty room, shivering now and again in the air-conditioned chill. She watched the spectacular sunset from habit, hardly even noticing when the great swollen sun finally sank those last few inches into the Gulf. It was only when the courtyard lights blinked on that she realized it was almost dark and that she'd been standing at the same window for nearly an hour, staring at nothing.

"This is ridiculous!" She said it out loud just to fill the silence, turning away and padding into the den. It was friendlier in here, done in browns and golds and polished oak, but tonight it didn't feel any more appealing than the rest of the apartment. She wandered across to the television and turned it on, watched a game show for a moment or two then spun the dial slowly, finding nothing that caused even a flicker of interest. A quick check of the videotape shelf had the same effect. She realized that for the first time in a long while she didn't want to be alone.

You can always invite Brett out for a pizza and beer, she reminded herself. Or for that matter, you could tell Hunter you changed your mind. She glanced at the clock. It was still early. Maybe she'd just go out to dinner herself. She could take Brett's horror novel and settle into a booth at the Old Post Office Deli with a basket of shrimp and a pot of tea, surrounded by the chatter of cheerful voices, laughter and country and western music.

Her spirits lifted at the thought, and she smiled, feeling suddenly better. "That's it!" she told herself, striding into the bedroom to change. "And a big slice of carrot cake just to round the evening out." It wouldn't be the most exciting evening she'd ever spent, she had to admit, but it sure beat sitting around here feeling sorry for herself.

Hunter was trying to adjust the temperature of his bath water, when someone knocked. He swore with considerable feeling and turned the tap off, then grabbed a towel and wrapped it around his hips on his way to the door.

"Yeah?" He wrenched the door open irritably and found himself staring into a pair of startled chocolate-brown eyes. "Well, I'll be damned," he added quite sincerely, feeling just about as surprised as Jill looked.

She blinked, then smiled hesitantly and gestured with the pizza carton. "I . . . uh . . . didn't feel like going out to dinner, but I didn't feel like eating alone, either. It . . . I mean, if you had other plans or anything . . ."

"Get in here," he growled good-naturedly, reaching out and taking the six-pack of beer from her other hand. "Since when did you start drinking this stuff?"

She shrugged as she stepped by him, looking ill at ease. "It seemed like the right thing to go with pizza." She stood there uneasily for a moment or two, then suddenly wheeled around and strode back toward the door, eyes desperate. "Look, this wasn't such a good idea. I should have phoned first. You're probably busy and—"

"It's a good idea," Hunter told her calmly, not moving from in front of the door.

"But . . ."

"I hope you didn't get olives on this thing."

She shook her head, still looking panic-stricken. "No olives, no anchovies, double cheese. Just the way you like it."

He slipped the pizza out of her hands with an appreciative sniff and nodded toward the living room. "Go on in and sit down. I'll pull on a pair of pants and grab a couple of plates, and dinner will be served."

"I could come back," she said quickly, giving him a hopeful look. She gestured at the towel. "I mean, if you want to shower, I could—"

"Hey," he said with a quiet laugh, "will you relax? I can take a shower anytime." He tossed the pizza onto the counter and walked across to where she was standing, her eyes still wide and frightened. "I don't bite, Jill. You should know that by now."

"I know." She backed away, looking trapped. "I...oh, hell!" She lifted her arms in a gesture of defeat, then let them fall to her sides. "I don't even know what I'm doing here. One minute I was driving by the pizza place, the next I was standing outside your door." She looked around at him in despair, then laughed and shook her head. "I was going to sneak away and pretend I'd never been here, except it would take me a week to eat that thing by myself."

"I'm glad you came."

Her expression softened and she smiled again, still hesitantly but without the utter panic that had been there before. "So am I."

Watching her, he thought of that first night together. She'd been as frightened as a deer then, too, not knowing what to say or where to look. The awareness, the sexual tension between them, had been growing all afternoon, and although they'd both known the evening's outcome was inevitable, they'd still played the game of coffee and conversation. Finally their eyes had met and held, the unworded question hanging in the air. He'd gotten up and had picked her up in his arms without a word, carrying her into the bedroom where he'd slowly undressed her, then had gently,

sweetly made love to her. Afterward, smiling that secret little woman smile of utter contentment, she'd nestled against
him as though she'd always belonged there.

That same tension was between them now, as vital and
urgent as if those seven intervening months had never happened. He could tell that she felt it, too, and as her velvet
eyes locked with his, he felt himself spun back through time
with a wrench that made him catch his breath.

Paralyzed, Jill watched Hunter move toward her. He
seemed much bigger than she remembered, naked shoulders as solid as concrete against the light behind him, face
intent, almost dangerous. She put her hands out to ward
him off, touching warm flesh. Fingers splayed against his
chest, she held him at bay, staring wide-eyed up at him. "I
had a feeling this might be a mistake," she whispered
breathlessly. But even as she spoke, her fingers slipped up
to his shoulders and drew him nearer. "A big mistake..."

Hunter paused with his mouth inches from hers, curved
in a smile. He put his hands on her hips and pulled her
firmly against him. "And I have a feeling," he murmured
huskily, "that you've never been more wrong."

Six

"Hunter..."

"Tell me." His lips brushed hers, teasing them apart. "Tell me what I want to hear, Jill."

"Oh, no..." It was no more than a sigh as she slowly relaxed into the remembered warmth of his embrace. But her lips were already opening for his kiss and when the tip of his tongue touched hers coaxingly, she drew it deeply into her mouth.

A shudder ran through him and he tightened his hands on her back, a groan escaping. His mouth possessed hers with the fierce urgency of a man too long denied and Jill felt her self-control start to slip as her own needs burst into flame. The taste of his desire filled her mouth and she whimpered softly, feeling the vital thrust of his body.

That explicit response had frightened her once. It was so blatant, so uncompromisingly male, and he'd made no effort to hide it from her. But he'd been patient with her fears;

he'd given her all the time she needed to feel comfortable with his body while leisurely teaching her to be comfortable with her own. And soon she'd reveled in it, loving his need for her as much as she loved him. She moved her hips against him now, suddenly wanting him so badly she was aching, and Hunter took a sharp, indrawn breath of near-pain. He covered her mouth with his again and again, both demanding and coaxing.

"My God, Jill," he spoke between kisses, his tongue flickering, nuzzling, "I haven't closed my eyes once in seven months without seeing you, touching you. For the last two days I haven't been able to think of anything but making you mine again, of being inside you."

Jill tried to turn her mouth away from his but couldn't, finding herself nibbling his lip instead. "Oh, Hunter, this isn't . . . I don't think this is why I came over here."

"Yes, it is," he murmured against her mouth, curling his hands around her bottom possessively and gently kneading her. "This is exactly why you came over here tonight. You love me, remember? This is what people in love do . . ." He bent his knees slightly and lifted her, fitting himself intimately between her thighs.

Jill shuddered and clung desperately to him. "But I don't love you," she protested weakly. "I don't even *like* you most of the time."

Hunter laughed that deep, rumbly laugh she loved, biting and nuzzling the tender spot under her ear until she was ready to faint. "Love doesn't always make sense, Jill. You can't put love in a test tube and break it down into all its elements and match it against a chart. Love just . . . is."

And that, Jill thought with a little inward sigh of satisfaction, was something she couldn't argue. Something she didn't *want* to argue. She loved this impossible, stubborn, bullheaded man heart and soul, and it was pointless trying to deny it. Even if her mind tried to convince her of its impossibility, her heart and body told her otherwise. It felt so right, letting herself simply relax into the spiraling magic of his mouth, hands and body. Coming back into his arms was like coming home, and she felt all the anger and bitterness within her start to dissolve, and the tightness around her heart give way.

"I do love you," she whispered against his mouth. "How did I ever think I'd stopped loving you?"

"Because I hurt you." Hunter's voice was rough with emotion. "Because sometimes I get so caught up in what I do that I lose sight of the things that are important." He kissed her slowly and deeply, as though imprinting the essence of her on his heart. "I love you, Jill Benedict. Coming down here and telling you that has been the most terrifying thing I've ever done in my life, but it was do that or lose you forever. Just promise me that you'll never walk out of my life again. No matter what happens, we can solve it. If you just remember I love you more than anything in this world."

"Show me," she whispered, tangling her fingers in his hair and pulling him down for another kiss. "Show me how much, Hunt."

"Now?" he purred, his hands already on the drawstring of her slacks. He tugged the knot free and slowly started loosening the waist. "Tell me how exactly, Jill."

"As exactly as humanly possible," she coaxed with a breathless little laugh, slowly insinuating the fingers of both hands under the upper edge of the towel still clinging precariously to his hips. A gentle tug was all it took.

"You always did like unwrapping presents, didn't you?"

"The ones you brought me." She caressed his chest, kissing him lightly. "I've been thinking about you all day."

"Thinking about what?"

"About this. About all the things you taught me."

"You were an excellent student."

"My father always told me not to waste a good education."

"Your father probably wouldn't approve of this particular curriculum."

"He teaches anatomy, remember? Basic biology..."

"I love studying anatomy and biology with you," Hunter whispered. "And chemistry. We make such great chemistry together."

"Are you going to stand here making bad puns all night, or are you going to—?"

"The latter, my darling," Hunter whispered. "Very definitely the latter."

Hunter eased the slacks over her hips and let them fall to the floor. "These are a big improvement over those jeans you used to wear. It used to take me an hour to get you peeled out of them."

"I got the impression you enjoyed the peeling."

"I di-did." Hunter flinched, breath hissing, as she set her teeth gently around one hard nipple and flicked her tongue across it. "But I don't think I can wait that long this time. In fact, I don't know if I'm even going to last long enough to get you out of this." *This* was her cream-colored bikini, and he ran his hands down her hips slowly, slipping his thumbs under the lace trim of the high-cut legs and following it downward and inward.

Jill went very still, biting her lip to keep from crying out when he gently, delicately, touched the very heart of her. It was like ice and fire, pleasure so intense it was close to pain, and she drew in a startled breath, feeling as though she were going to shatter into a million pieces.

"You're trembling."

"I'm...I'm afraid of what's..."

But Hunter just laughed softly, cradling her against him. "Always the scientist, observing and analyzing. Send the biochemist out to lunch, Jill. Let yourself feel every sensation, every touch. Don't think about what's happening, just let it happen."

And she did, taking a deep shuddering breath at the first intrusive touch, feeling the first tiny little spasms start, knowing by the change in his breathing that he could sense them, too. "It's been so long for you, too, hasn't it?" he whispered, his touch changing suddenly to a firm, insistent caress so perfectly attuned to her that the crystal-sharp tension built dizzyingly, started to splinter, spilled hot and urgent through her with such explosive force that she cried out.

She went limp against him, stunned by the power of that release. "That wasn't supposed to happen," she protested. "Not so soon!"

"Seven months is a long time to wait," Hunter whispered against her ear.

"It's cheating!" she declared, struggling to catch her breath.

"Don't stop to analyze it, Jill, just relax and enjoy. There's no such thing as too soon or too late. I love making it good for you. I've been dreaming all day of making it so good for you...."

"But we haven't—"

"We will."

"But you—"

"Soon," he murmured, stripping her lace bikini off swiftly. "Much too soon, in fact. Those seven months have been like seven years." He fumbled with the buttons on her blouse even as they started walking backward toward the sofa, then tossed it aside, closely followed by her bra. "I have a feeling," he whispered as he sank down onto the sofa and pulled her down over him, "that this may be over all too soon."

"Don't analyze it," Jill murmured, kneeling astride him. She cradled his head in her hands and smiled. "Just relax, my love, and enjoy it."

Hunter's eyes widened. "Jill, I was going to make love to—you." The last word was an astonished groan as she eased herself down onto him, so ready for him that even after seven long months there was no more than the slightest pressure before she enveloped him with silken ease.

"Do you mind if I make love to you instead?" she whispered, running her fingertips lightly down his chest, following the dense swirls of hair as it narrowed at his stomach. He threw his head back in agonized delight, eyes closed, teeth clenched and bared, his fingers tightening spasmodically on her hips. She could feel him tremble as he fought for control, taking her own satisfaction out of watching him respond so vitally to her every move.

"Mind?" he managed to gasp. "Darling, I am completely and utterly yours."

"I want it all," she breathed, arching her back and pressing herself down over him as completely as she could. He murmured a protest and she silenced his concern with a deep, drugging kiss that he responded to greedily, his tongue hot against hers.

He groaned something, lifting his hips and moving with growing urgency, and Jill tightened her thighs on his, feeling that deliciously familiar tension start to build within her again. She tried to ignore it, knowing that Hunter couldn't possibly control his own needs long enough to fan those embers to flame. Not that it mattered. Just being with him again, belonging to him so unconditionally like this, was satisfaction enough.

She opened her eyes to find him watching her, his narrowed gaze burning into hers, and a moment later he slipped his hand between them, touching her so intimately that it literally took her breath away. It brought her that last distance so swiftly that it made her head spin. At the last moment she surrendered herself completely to it, letting the flame wash through her in wave after searing wave until she didn't think she could stand anymore, but finding she could. It ebbed slowly, leaving her shaken and breathless, and she collapsed into Hunter's arms, tasting tears and not knowing whether they were hers or his.

"Oh, I love you," she whispered, burying her face in his neck. "Hunter, don't ever leave me."

"There's a better chance of the sun not coming up tomorrow," Hunter murmured. "I'm thirty-eight years old, Jill. I've seen things no man should ever see in a civilized world, and I hope that by writing about them I've helped make sure they'll never be seen again. I've done some things I'm proud of and a few I'm not. I'm probably no great prize as far as prizes go, but I love you. That's all I have to offer you, Jill. It's all I've got."

Jill smiled against his shoulder. "And I'm a twenty-seven-year-old, unemployed biochemist who'll probably never work in the field again, equally stubborn, far more idealistic, and at philosophical odds with practically everything you say. But I love you, too." She raised her head to look at him and caressed his cheek with her fingertips. "Do you think we have a chance, Kincaide?"

"I don't think we have a choice. We fit together too well." He grinned and ran his hands down her hips, pressing her into his lap. "And I don't mean just like this, although there's a lot to be said for it. I mean in all ways."

So he felt it, too, Jill marveled. She'd never fully realized how complete he made her life until she'd left Chapel Hill.

At first she'd thought the feeling of incompleteness she'd experienced was because she had no research project awaiting her when she got here. But it had been deeper than that.

Slowly she realized that it wasn't just her work she missed, but the time she'd spent with Hunter. She missed the long hours of relaxed conversation, the arguments, articles they'd read aloud together, the reminiscences. She missed sharing the dreams, the insecurities, the doubts, the laughter and the loving.

But most of all she missed just having him *there*—the quiet times when they'd both be busy at their own work and she'd glance up and see him frowning over his typewriter in the eternal search for the right word. Or sometimes she'd be deeply involved in something of her own when she'd suddenly become aware that he was watching her. They'd trade a smile, then go back to work, secure in the other's loving presence.

"You fit into my life pretty nicely, too."

"And your work here?" He asked it softly, holding her gaze. "How big a part of your life is it now?"

"It keeps me busy. Why?"

"If I asked you to come up to Washington and live with me, would it cause a major problem?"

Jill stared at him. "I . . . guess not."

"You don't look too sure."

Jill gave an astonished laugh. "Hunter, twenty minutes ago I was standing outside your door with a pizza, terrified to even—the pizza! I barely got in the door before . . . well, before this happened." Jill felt a blush spill across her cheeks. She gave a sputter of laughter and slipped her arms around his neck.

"Keep wriggling around like that," Hunter murmured as he nuzzled her ear, "and it's going to happen again. Soon."

"Really?" Jill ran the tip of her tongue around the inner curl of Hunter's ear, getting a response so immediate and strong that she gave a murmur of surprise.

Hunter chuckled. "Does that answer your question?"

"The pizza's getting cold."

"It's the only thing around here that is." Hunter ran his hands lightly down the backs of Jill's thighs, then held her tightly against him as he shifted so he was lying full-length on the sofa with Jill under him. He started kissing her, very slowly and leisurely. "That pizza's going to be a lot colder before we get around to it," he promised in a rusty growl. "The first time was just a bit of spontaneous combustion, all fireworks, but very little substance. But this time, my love, we're going to get down to some very serious chemistry."

"I have all night," Jill whispered, lifting her mouth to his.

It was nearly two hours later before Jill remembered the pizza again. She lay in Hunter's arms, warm and sleepy and pleasantly exhausted, every atom in her body still gently vibrating from the aftermath of their lovemaking. His breath stirred her hair and she looked up at him, smiling.

Hunter's face broke into a lazy grin. "How was that?"

"Unbelievable."

"So were you."

Jill felt herself blush. "You always were able to bring out the courtesan in me, but I never thought I could be so greedy." She touched his shoulder gently. "You look like you've been through a war. I didn't realize how tightly I was holding you at the end. You're scratched."

"I think I'll live," he assured her with a chuckle. "And it was worth every mark just to be able to watch you respond to me like that." His grin widened. "Do you know that when you blush, you turn pink all the way down to your—"

"Toes," Jill completed hastily, although Hunter's loving gaze wasn't anywhere near her feet. "And you knew I was the original blushing violet when you met me in Chapel Hill."

"When I met you in Chapel Hill, you struck me as being about the furthest thing from a blushing violet as I'd ever met. In fact, you intimidated the hell out of me. You were beautiful, self-confident, frighteningly bright. It was obvious that everyone there respected you, you even had the press corps eating out of your hands." He smiled, his eyes sparkling with mischief. "It was only when I got you out of that lab coat that I discovered you weren't quite the worldly lady I'd suspected."

Jill gave a peal of laughter. "Worldly? Me? I look self-confident in the lab because I am. I'm good at what I do. But outside that lab, Hunter Kincaide, you intimidated the hell out of *me*. I felt so out of my depth I didn't even know which way to swim!"

"You still haven't really answered my question." Hunter kissed the end of her nose. "Is Washington going to be a problem for you? We can always live somewhere else."

"Washington's no more of a problem than anywhere else." Jill sighed. "I haven't really thought about my future, but I'm going to have to pretty soon: My career as a biochemist is over. I can't just live here rent free, making grocery money taking blood samples from alligators and weighing mud turtles, and I won't live with you unless I can pay my way. I've got to decide what I want to do with my life, Hunter. Go back to school, get a job.... I have no idea. Biochemistry is all I know."

"There was one small catch about living with me," Hunter said very carefully. He was surprised to realize his heart was pounding, and his palms felt damp. Jill gazed up at him questioningly. "I want you to marry me, too."

She blinked. Opened her mouth to say something, closed it again. Frowned. "Oh, wow," she finally breathed, looking stunned.

Hunter gave a snort of laughter. "That from a woman who can talk for half an hour and not use a word under fifteen syllables." But Jill didn't smile. Instead, her frown grew even deeper, and Hunter felt his stomach pull tight.

"Oh, Hunter," she sighed. She slipped her arms around him and snuggled closer.

"Jill," Hunter said slowly, "you're going to have to be plainer than that. Does this mean yes, no or maybe?"

"It means I love you very much, but your timing's not very good." It was Hunter's turn to frown.

Jill pulled back to look up at him. "I can't marry you, Hunter. Not yet. Not until the Ethics Committee has made their decision, not until you've finished your series. If we get married now, it's going to look as though we're both moving over to the other side. Having a wife who's being investigated for the same kind of research fraud you're writing about isn't going to do much for your impartiality. And being married to the man who uncovered that mess at Phoenix isn't going to endear me to the Ethics people, either. They're going to wonder if anything really did happen at Phoenix, or if I simply faked a fraud to give you something to write about."

"To hell with the series, and to hell with the Ethics Review Committee, too," Hunter growled. "I want to marry you, Jill. I want to wake up every morning and see you lying beside me. I want to have kids before it's too late, and live like a normal human being for the first time in my life."

Jill started to laugh and cupped his face in her hands. "Hunt, I didn't say I wouldn't marry you. I just said not right now. A few months, that's all I'm asking. It'll give us time to get to know each other again. And we'll have kids before it's too late, I promise." She blushed again. "Who knows, we may have started things already."

Hunter's heart did a fast cartwheel. "You're not on—?"

She shook her head, not looking at him. "You took care of things in Chapel Hill. I was planning to get a prescription, but after I left, it didn't exactly seem . . . well, necessary. There's been no one down here. . . ."

"Damn it, Jill, I'm sorry." Hunter could cheerfully have kicked himself. Thirty-eight years old, he told himself angrily, and still in too damned much of a hurry to think about something as basic as contraception! "I should have made sure before—is it going to worry you?" It was going to worry *him*, Hunter knew. Not that he didn't want a baby—Jill's baby—but she had enough things on her mind right now without being pregnant, too, and he vowed to be careful from now on.

"Not in the least," she said with a smile. "My mother was just asking me when I was planning on making her a grandmother. She didn't seem concerned about the fact I didn't have a man in my life. I think she figures I'll just pop by the lab one day and brew something up in a test tube."

Hunter had to laugh. "Not a chance! I've got nothing against test tubes, and making babies the old-fashioned way may be as inefficient as hell, but it's sure more fun."

"As a biochemist with a degree in biogenetics, I should be disagreeing with you. But as a woman . . ." She smiled. "As a woman, Mr. Kincaide, I agree with you wholeheartedly."

"Let's go to bed."

Her eyes widened. "Hunter! You can't possibly be serious."

He grinned, then gave her a long kiss. "What I had in mind was tossing that pizza in the microwave, grabbing a quick shower and a shave, then curling up in bed with pizza, two cold beers and a handful of video movies.'' His grin widened. ''Then, after a bit of recuperative R and R, who knows what might happen.''

''That's what I love about you, Kincaide,'' Jill said with a delighted laugh. ''You've got real class. Pizza, beer and bed.''

''Would you rather go out to dinner? I'm not adverse to Lobster Thermidor, a good wine and some dancing. If you wish to be wooed, my lady, wooed you shall be.''

''No.'' Jill sat up and kissed him soundly, then got to her feet and picked up his discarded towel, wrapping it modestly around her. ''Pizza, beer and bed sounds just fine, Kincaide. And last one to the shower has to wash the dishes!''

Jill awoke with something kissing the back of her left knee. She smiled sleepily and wriggled her toes, filled with such a delicious feeling of contentment that she felt like purring. The kisses slowly worked their way up the back of her thigh, then over the curve of her bottom where they paused for a delightful moment or two at the base of her spine before continuing their way leisurely upward. They settled at the nape of her neck, then worked their way around to her ear.

''I can't remember the last time I've been awakened so delightfully,'' she murmured as a large, warm and unmistakably male body settled tightly along her back.

''About three this morning, I think,'' came the throaty reply. Two hands slipped around her waist and started caressing her breasts and stomach. Then there was a husky laugh, and Hunter hugged her fiercely. ''I also think I'm dreaming if I think this is going to lead anywhere. You wore me out, darlin'.''

"Who wore who out?" she protested. "I was just lying here minding my own business all night. Every time I got nicely asleep, some maniac would start making love to me."

"I seem to recall some other maniac begging him not to stop." He gave her a gentle swat on the rump and slid out of bed. "Do you have to go to work this morning?"

"Should." She stared blearily at Hunter's travel clock. "That can't be right."

"Eight-thirty." Hunter's grin was pure devilry. "Want me to call Douglass and tell him you overslept?"

"Don't you men ever get tired of trying to one-up each other at absolutely everything? No wonder we have wars."

"It's called keeping the competitive edge, sweetheart," he called over his shoulder as he headed for the bathroom.

"It's called gloating." She sat up and yawned. The shower came on a minute or two later, and she could hear Hunter whistling. Yawning again, she slid out of bed and pulled on a shirt that was hanging on the doorknob, then made her way into the kitchen and turned on the automatic coffee maker.

She smiled. Just like a wife, she mused. What would it be like, being married? Lying naked in Hunter's arms every night, waking up with him already making love to her, the long, powerful thrusts of his body bringing her such dizzying pleasure that she cried out again and again, arching and moving under him as he coaxed her over that bright, final release. What would it be like carrying his child? She smiled again, laying her hand on her flat stomach. It gave her shivers just to think of it.

She left the coffee maker burbling to itself and wandered into the dining room, munching on an oatmeal cookie she'd found in the cupboard. The table was laden with stacks of paper, books and boxes of computer disks, and a compact computer and printer rose from the clutter. Jill felt the back of her neck prickle and she cast a quick glance toward the corridor leading to the bedroom. Hunter was still in the shower, singing lustily over the sound of the water.

Jill looked at the computer again. All his notes on Phoenix Research would be in there somewhere, telling all he wouldn't: details, names, what he knew, what he suspected.

You can't! she told herself firmly. You can't root through his private notes like a cat burglar. All you have to do is ask him and he'll tell you.

Except that would lead to his asking questions, too. Questions she couldn't answer. Questions she *wouldn't* answer.

"Oh, hell." She closed her eyes, the cookie suddenly like dust in her mouth. How in heaven's name could she marry Hunter, not only having lied to him, but harboring that lie forever?

Hunter was whistling again, enthusiastically off-key. Jill glanced at the corridor again, then, feeling like a thief, she sat on the edge of the chair and looked swiftly through a pile of computer disks. She found one labeled Phoenix and stared at it, feeling cold and a little sick. Then she took a deep breath, slipped the disk into the computer, and turned it on.

It took her a heart-stopping moment or two to figure the system out, and then she promptly ran into a brick wall when she tried to call up the list of files on the Phoenix disk. She stared at the screen, her pulse racing, and swore under her breath.

Password?

She wet her lips again, part of her wanting to tear the disk out of the machine and pretend she'd never even thought of doing this. But another part of her suddenly wanted desperately to read those notes. Taking another deep breath, she tried a couple of words at random, Hunter's name, the name of his old newspaper, variations on the words *Phoenix* and *Research*. Nothing. The word glowed back at her, as resolute as stone.

"Open, damn you." Whimsically, she typed *Sesame*, not really surprised when it didn't work. Next, she tried *Jill*, then *Benedict*, both with no result. Why in heaven's name did he have to be so cryptic! Then, with nothing else to lose, she typed in *Boston*. And watched the screen silently unfold before her.

"*Now* what?" She stared at the long list of files in despair. "How on earth am I supposed to unravel this mess?"

"If you tell me what you're looking for," Hunter said quietly from behind her, "I could tell you which file to call up."

Seven

Jill leaped to her feet, knocking a pile of papers off the table. File folders went flying in all directions, spilling their contents across the floor. She stared at Hunter in horror, a hot blush pouring across her cheeks. "I—it—that is, I was just . . ." She gestured aimlessly, knowing it was readily apparent what she was doing. "This isn't what it looks like, Hunter."

Hunter stood leaning against the door frame, dressed in a pair of pale-blue cotton slacks and a loose-fitting white linen shirt that made him look more like a pirate than a journalist. Somehow, Jill didn't find the similarity at all reassuring.

"I—" Jill gazed at him desperately, then dropped into the chair, shoulders slumping. "Yes, it is. What it looks like, I mean."

To her surprise, Hunter laughed softly. He pushed himself indolently away from the door frame and strolled across to the table. "Déjà vu."

Jill looked up at him hesitantly, remembering walking into her office at Phoenix to find Hunter sitting at her computer console, casually going through the personnel files of every employee there. She'd never discovered how he'd breached the system security, but she did know how he'd gotten into the lab and her console. The proof had been there in front of him: her own coded door card, taken from her wallet; a visitor identification badge she'd given him on the first day and had carelessly forgotten to take back; a scrap of paper with her computer access codes on it, hastily copied from her notebook. Now, seven months later, she was guilty of the same crime.

"Hunter, I'm sorry," she whispered. "We keep making liars out of each other. And thieves."

"I never lied to you, Jill." His eyes held hers firmly.

Guilt shot through her, hot as flame. She looked away, unable to hold his gaze.

"What do you want to know, sweetheart?" Hunter squatted beside her. He put one hand between her shoulder blades and started rubbing it in soothing circles as he adjusted the brightness on the computer screen. "Jill?"

"I don't even know. I just saw the computer and all your notes, and wondered what you'd found at Phoenix. That's...all." It wasn't, of course, and Jill could see by his eyes that he knew it was far from all.

Hunter leaned forward to kiss her, then stood up. "Why don't you go and have your shower and get dressed while I make breakfast, then we can sit down and go over the whole thing."

"Hunt—"

"Go." Hunter smiled and pushed her gently toward the door. He watched Jill walk slowly away, then turned the computer off and walked into the kitchen. Was she ready to talk about it? he wondered as he sliced a grapefruit in half and started sectioning it. She'd kept it bottled up for seven months, and it was eating away at her like acid. He could see it in her eyes, in the drawn look on her face. And there was absolutely nothing he could do until she decided to talk it out.

For half an instant he found himself wondering if that damned computer was why she was here. Just how desperate was she to find out what he knew about Phoenix? he brooded. Enough to spend the night with him, enough to...?

He caught his rambling thoughts and shook his head impatiently. Jill couldn't even look him in the eye and admit she'd been guilty at Phoenix; she certainly wasn't capable of deliberately seducing him to get access to his notes. Besides, he reminded himself with a comfortable inward smile, no woman on earth could pretend last night's passion. Whatever whim had sent her rummaging through his computer this morning, it had been love that had brought her into his arms last night.

He found himself grinning, wondering when it was going to hit him that he was halfway to being married. He'd sworn years ago that marriage was one experience he had no intention of repeating, and he'd spent a good many years avoiding it with no problem at all. Yet here he was, more in love than he'd ever been in his life, talking about children and settling down without even a twinge of doubt. Maybe that's all he'd needed, he reflected: time, and the right woman. Maybe that's what he'd been looking for during all those years of wandering.

He was so deep in thought that he didn't hear the shower go off, and he didn't realize that Jill had rejoined him until he turned to carry the two bowls of grapefruit sections and a plate of buttered toast into the living room. She was sitting on the sofa, one bare foot tucked under her. Chin planted in one palm, she was staring out the glass doors leading to the small balcony.

Hunter slid the doors open and set the food on the table outside, then stepped back into the room. "Eggs and Canadian bacon okay? It's all I've got on hand." Jill was frowning now, obviously as lost in thought as he'd been, and he whistled to catch her attention. She blinked, then looked at him as though surprised to find him there. "Breakfast?" he queried again.

She shook her head. "Just coffee, thanks. I'm not hungry."

Hunter thought about arguing with her, then subsided with a nod and walked back into the kitchen to get the coffeepot and two mugs. Patience, my friend, he told himself. The only way she could get rid of the pain and guilt was to admit that she was covering up for someone at Phoenix. And *that* meant saying who really had fiddled with the documentation on that MS project. Which was something she'd already made abundantly clear she had no intention of doing.

"Come on outside," he told her quietly and she nodded and got to her feet, following him.

The big screened balcony was the most comfortable part of the condominium, as far as Hunter was concerned, and since he'd arrived he'd spent as much time out there as the heat would allow. It was a jungle of greenery and blooming tropical flowers, attractively furnished with white wicker and wrought iron, and it overlooked the beach. He pulled out one of the pink-and-green cushioned chairs for her, then sat down himself and poured two mugs of steaming coffee.

"Where do you want to start?"

Jill looked uncomfortable, avoiding his eyes as she nibbled at a piece of toast.

Hunter leaned back in the chair and set his foot on the edge of the balcony railing, taking a cautious sip of coffee. He eyed Jill, trying to decide on the best approach. She wasn't eating the toast so much as toying with it and as he watched her a stray breeze ruffled her hair. She looked lost and uncertain sitting there, such a far cry from the self-assured scientist he'd known in Chapel Hill that it made his heart ache.

"It was DeRocher, wasn't it?" he said. "And Preston Neals."

A frown crossed her forehead, fleetingly. She picked up the spoon and poked at the grapefruit segments. "Don't you read your own press, Hunter?" She glanced up at him with a flash of the old Jill Benedict spirit. "I did it, remember?"

A jolt of raw impatience shot through Hunter, impatience at the games they were playing, at Jill's obstinacy. He tamped it down firmly. "If you know what happened, why were you going through my notes?"

She looked down, cheeks turning pink under the tan. "I wanted to make sure you had it right."

"Oh, I think I have it right, Jill." She looked at him sharply, and he smiled. "I'll run it by you and if I'm missing anything, you can fill it in." She didn't say anything, although her eyes narrowed slightly. Hunter relaxed and placed his other foot on the balcony railing and crossed his ankles. "Phoenix Research was set up about fifteen years ago as a tax shelter by Howard Ackerton, Senior. The old man had watched one of his sons die of cancer, and he decided to develop a privately funded research lab that could afford to hire the best people in the field and turn them loose. The idea was that if you took brilliant people and gave them unlimited money so they didn't have to run around trying to find funding, you'd have a cure for cancer in five years.''

"Which didn't happen," Jill said quietly.

"Not yet. But the idea was sound. The only problem was that after Ackerton, Senior died eight years ago and Ackerton, Junior took over, the original concept changed. One of the first things to bite the dust was Senior's belief that Phoenix was purely altruistic. Junior's bottom line was profit—to hell with humanitarianism, find us something that'll make us a bundle. Research teams were expected to produce results, not vague possibilities.

"Ackerton still poured money into getting the top brains in the business and providing them with all the newest toys, but they were expected to pay their way. At the moment, Phoenix has six teams in-house. One is working on cancer, the others on AIDS, diabetes and a half dozen other things. And Team Four—your team—which was working on slow cells or whatever.''

"Viruses," Jill corrected with the ghost of a smile. "Didn't you ever read all those articles I gave you?''

"Sure I read 'em, I just didn't understand more than one word out of every twelve." He gave her a quick grin. "By the time they brought you on last year, Team Four was in trouble. They'd been working flat out for more than two years and were close to a breakthrough, but not close enough to satisfy the Ackerton warlords who handle the purse strings. Team Four was given one year. If they didn't have something major to show by then, funding would be cut off.''

"Reallocated," Jill said. "The money would have been diverted to Roberta Wu's AIDS team.''

Hunter nodded. Jill didn't seem threatened by talking about things that were common knowledge, and she was even starting to open up a bit. But what would happen when he went on to the next step? "After you joined Phoenix, Team Four's fortunes started to pick up. But not quickly enough for the powers that be." Hunter took a deep breath, deciding to plunge right in. "Simon DeRocher, son of a Nobel Prize winner and one of Harvard Medical School's best, started to panic. Team Four was his baby, his chance to beat even his daddy's brilliant record, and he was damned if he was going to lose it all when he was that close."

Jill's eyes were wary, but she made no move to either support or deny his allegations. Hunter took another sip of coffee, his mind racing as he tried to decide how to continue. Right down the middle, he told himself. He'd pussy-footed around the topic for too long, and he was sick of it. "DeRocher needed something to convince the Board to extend funding for another year. From his viewpoint, he wouldn't really be lying, just manipulating the truth a bit. Another year's funding would provide the time to come up with the real breakthrough. All he was doing was buying time."

Jill had gone very still, her eyes watchful and alert. Hunter put his coffee mug down. "As Team Leader, DeRocher was in the best position to do it. The fewer people involved, the less chance of a leak. He'd just fiddle the results a bit, make it appear that you were a lot closer to finding a cure than you really were. But he couldn't do it alone. The Director of Labs—Preston Neals—*had* to have known about it. Maybe even approved it."

Hunter paused, swearing silently as he saw Jill's eyes shutter. Too close, he realized. He'd trod just a little too close to the truth, and she'd pulled into her shell. He eased his feet to the floor and leaned forward, reaching across to put his hand on one of Jill's. It was ice-cold and he folded his around it. "Jill, I know Neals was involved. So was DeRocher. And at least one other. John Conyers, I think. Everyone, it seems, but you." She didn't say anything, wouldn't even look at him, and Hunter swore under his breath. "Talk to me, Jill."

"You already seem to have everything you want to know."

"Not by half." He stared at her impatiently, willing her to talk. But it was going to take more than mental urging to get her to open up. "Why have you kept your mouth shut about this so long when you weren't even involved?"

She impatiently tossed her head, her expression annoyed now. "Who says I wasn't, Kincaide? Everyone else thinks I was."

"Because I have proof you weren't." She shot him a wary look, and he smiled at her. "I have a copy of a confidential memo sent to Neals from one of the members of Team Four two days after the announcement had been made. The memo suggests—no, *demands* that an investigation be made into what the author called 'possible inconsistencies' in the test data." He held her startled gaze triumphantly. "The author of that memo was Dr. Jill Benedict. You knew damned well that your team hadn't made any breakthrough. You're too good not to have known. And there's no way you had the slightest thing to do with it yourself."

Jill had to fight to catch her breath, knowing she'd gone pale. How in God's name had he gotten hold of that memo? He'd obviously been hard at work during the past seven months, she thought angrily. Just what other little surprises had he uncovered? Hunter's gaze held hers, determination etched in every line of his face, and Jill felt her heart drop. It was worse than she'd thought: Bulldog Kincaide didn't just have his teeth embedded firmly in this story, he'd made Phoenix his own personal vendetta.

And suddenly, she felt all the fight drain out of her. She was so sick of the charade she'd been playing for seven months, sick of the lies, the games. "Neals wasn't involved," she whispered. "He didn't even know what was going on, not until I sent that memo. And even then, he didn't believe it." She heard Hunter ease out a tightly held breath and looked up, seeing relief wash across those rugged features.

But there was impatience there, too. "So DeRocher was behind it?" She nodded. "Alone?"

"John Conyers was in on it. And Poul Wilczek, too, I think."

Hunter nodded slowly, his eyes glowing with the old fire. "So I was right!" He lunged to his feet and started pacing, his face animated. "What the hell made them take the risk? Money? Fame?"

"Both." Jill closed her eyes and let her head fall back wearily. She felt almost light-headed with relief, finally talking about it openly after all this time. She opened her eyes again and looked at Hunter. "Phoenix Research is supposed to be independent of Ackerton Pharmaceutical control or interference. Ackerton, Senior had set it up so it received money from a separate trust created for just that purpose. The facility gets a generous annual budget, indexed for inflation, with provision made for extra funds to be available if something really promising turns up. Allocation of those funds among the various ongoing projects is supposed to be handled internally by a budgeting group consisting of Dr. Neals, all the Team Leaders and the head of Phoenix—Dean Ackerton."

Jill felt a surge of anger. "And that's where the problem is. Ackerton, Senior had specified that Phoenix was to be headed up by an independent Board, all of them scientists in their own right. He knew what would happen if the lab was controlled by businessmen who lacked the specialized knowledge or interest required to run a research facility. But the Ackerton family tossed the independent Board out two years ago and replaced it with one man, a loyal Ackerton son.''

"Whose bottom line is profit, not science."

Jill nodded. "Dean Ackerton wouldn't know an electron microscope from a toaster. He thinks you can simply order up a cure for a disease like you order up breakfast. And not just any old disease, either. It has to be a disease with lots of 'public appeal'—that's actually what he said, can you believe it? He wants his Phoenix teams working only on designer-label diseases that have lots of press appeal." She pushed the bowl of grapefruit away angrily. "Last year we got a request from a group of missionary doctors on some little island in southeast Asia who had come up with a workingman's cure for Hansen's Disease—leprosy. They'd concocted something out of tree bark and ground-up beetles or something that actually seemed to promote tissue regeneration. They asked us if we'd run this stuff through the lab, determine how and why it worked, and synthesize it for world distribution, no strings attached. They were *giving* us the stuff! Ackerton turned them down flat. He didn't think leprosy was something nice people wanted to talk about, and didn't want the Ackerton name attached to it."

"But Phoenix is working on AIDS, and that's sure as hell a disease nice people don't want to talk about."

Jill smiled bitterly. "But AIDS is high profile, with lots of publicity. And money. Whoever comes up with the cure for AIDS is going to make a killing."

Hunter swore wearily. "So much for philanthropy. It must have driven you crazy."

"It did. I ignored all the politics as best I could, but it affected everything we did. When Ackerton told us to pull the plug on the MS project because it didn't look promising, I swear I could have killed him." She leaned forward. "We were close, Hunter. Really close!"

"And that's when DeRocher decided to hurry things along."

"Simon hit the roof when Dr. Neals told us the Board's decision. But it wasn't because of our research—it was an ego thing with him. He was always impatient, wanting results but hating the time and work it takes to get them. He and Ackerton have a lot in common. He was always cutting corners, working something through ninety percent of the way, then rushing the last ten percent, which is usually where the work has to be the most precise. He'd repeat a test five times instead of ten, or jump whole sequences of steps because we'd done them before and he figured everything would run true. He hated what he called the Mickey Mouse details."

Jill smiled. "It's called Nobel Prize Fever, and it's all too pervasive among today's young hotshot researchers. They want dessert without having to wade through all the liver and onions to get there.

"Then there was the money. The 'prize' money." Another surge of anger shot through Jill and she narrowed her eyes. "That idiot Ackerton decided the way to *motivate* his Phoenix teams was to offer them an incentive. It was supposed to encourage competition, but at Phoenix competition among the teams was often so strong it actually interfered with our work. All the prize money did was inflame an already explosive situation." She gave him the ghost of a smile. "People think researchers are selfless seekers of truth and healing. I used to believe that myself.

But a lot of us are driven as much by ambition and ego as by any humanitarian reason. And greed.''

"Which was it with DeRocher?''

"Raw ambition.''

"And you found out what he was up to.''

"At first I thought it was a mistake. He was always leaping to monumental conclusions without taking the time to work them out. Sometimes I spent more lab time proving Simon wrong than I did actually working.'' Jill hesitated, not quite sure if she was on safe ground or not. She loved Hunter, and he deserved to know most of what happened at Phoenix, but there were some facts that could never come out.

"How did they keep you from finding out what was going on? They must have spent as much time and effort keeping you in the dark as they did actually falsifying research material.''

"Simon assigned me to some peripheral work. At first I thought it was his way of punishing me for riding him so hard, but when he leaked word of our supposed 'miracle discovery' to the press, I realized he'd gotten me out of the way so they could change results.'' She shook her head, the disbelief and rage still strong even after seven months.

"I knew damned well there hadn't been any 'miracle discovery.' I went to see him the night he went public and threatened to blow the whole thing wide open, to haul him up in front of an Ethics Committee and watch him sweat.'' She stopped, realizing she'd said too much. Realizing that she'd worked herself into a corner from which there may be no escape. Hunter's eyes fastened onto her, and Jill felt her heart drop.

"Why didn't you?''

She swallowed, shrugging with what she hoped was the right amount of casualness. "By then you'd started poking around, and I knew it was all going to come out anyway." Thin, she told herself, very thin. Hunter would never buy it. But it was the best she could do. Damn it, she wasn't cut out for this sort of thing, all the lying and the subterfuge!

Hunter frowned, staring down at her. "If you weren't involved, Jill, why didn't you come out and say so? You didn't owe DeRocher anything. Why take the blame while he, Conyers and Neals got off scot-free?"

Jill pushed her chair back and stood up. She walked across to the screened railing and looked out at the water. A wide band of sea oats, planted along the beach to prevent wind and sea from washing the sand away, waved their plumbed tips languorously in the light breeze. A triangular fin cut through the water just offshore and Jill watched it, eyes narrowed against the glitter of sunlight on the waves.

"What the hell!" Hunter breathed from just behind her. "Is that a shark?"

As if in reply, a long sleek shape crested the waves, then arched gracefully into the air. Another joined it, then two more, their plumbed exhalations rainbowing in the sun. "Porpoises," Jill said simply, shading her eyes. And suddenly the sea seemed alive with black torpedo shapes, all chasing each other and gamboling through the lazy waves like kittens after twine.

Above them, brown pelicans sailed stiff-winged. Now and again one would suddenly bank and drop in a fast dive, hitting the water in a cloud of spray. Jill always held her breath, expecting them to break their necks, but they unfailingly reappeared on the surface a moment or two later, bobbing around like giant bathtub toys. She could sense Hunter's presence right behind her, yet she still started slightly when he slipped his arms around her waist and tugged her against him.

He kissed the side of her throat, his breath moist and warm on her skin. "Jill, everything you've said so far fits in with what I know. But you still haven't told me why you didn't blow the lid off this thing seven months ago when your name was first involved, or who you're covering up for."

Jill drew in a deep breath and let it out again in a sigh, relaxing back against Hunter's solid chest. A tiny brilliant-green lizard scampered up one of the screening supports, pausing for a moment as though overwhelmed by the immensity of its world. Jill watched it with sympathy, feeling overwhelmed herself. She slid her hands over Hunter's and meshed her fingers with his. "What would you say if I asked you to just let it drop?" she asked him softly. "If I asked you to finish the series and forget you ever heard of Phoenix Research."

Hunter winced. He'd hoped she would never come out and ask him that directly. He'd asked it himself countless times, had laid awake nights trying to find the solution. "Are you?"

"Yes."

He was silent for even longer this time, wishing there was some other answer than the one he knew he had to give. "I can't, Jill," he said finally, his voice ragged. He rested his chin on the top of her head, cradling her tightly. "You know that."

"Yes." She sighed deeply, stepping out of his embrace and staring out across the water. "I guess I do."

"I'm sorry."

To his surprise, she smiled faintly. "Strange as it sounds, I believe you. You're like the Ancient Mariner, Hunt, with that damned Phoenix hanging around your neck like an albatross."

Hunter frowned, brooding silently. He'd had that same image himself now and again over the past seven months, feeling weighed down and haunted. Was he just doing his job, he found himself wondering, or had Phoenix become an obsession with him? There was a fine line between the two sometimes; he'd watched others stumble over it and lose themselves in the magnificent chaos of madness. He'd come close: sacrificing security, marriage, almost life itself in his unswerving determination to get the story.

"Jill, if DeRocher is blackmailing you, you have my sworn promise that I'll protect you." But she was looking out over the Gulf again, her mouth set, her stubborn chin as hard as granite. Hunter felt his temper start to rise in spite of his best efforts. "We're going to have one hell of a marriage if you pull this iron maiden act every time the word *Phoenix* comes up, lady."

She turned her head to look at him. "That can be remedied easily enough."

Hunter stared at her, his blood pressure slowly elevating. Then he gave an abrupt snort of laughter. "Oh, no, you don't! You're not playing those kinds of games with me, sweetheart. We're getting married, Phoenix or no Phoenix."

That worked. Her eyes widened and she stared at him indignantly. "Don't you try to bully me, Hunter Kincaide!"

"Then stop acting like such a damned fool!" he shot back. "I don't understand how a woman can be so frighteningly bright about some things, and so damned thickheaded about others!"

"If you've finished insulting me, I think I'll go to work." Jill strode around the table, back ramrod stiff.

But Hunter was there a step ahead of her. He leaned against the glass door leading back into the living room, holding it firmly closed. "It's Neals, isn't it?" he demanded. "Your good friend and mentor, the man who pulled strings to get you into Phoenix." She glared at him stonily. "He knew how good you were and he wanted you on his Phoenix teams. You were delighted to work with him again, even if it meant putting up with Simon DeRocher and Ackerton politics. I know you idolize the man, that as far as you're concerned he can walk on water."

"Dr. Neals is probably the single most brilliant mind in biochemistry today," Jill said through gritted teeth. "Yes, I was flattered when he wanted me to join Phoenix. And yes, I think he can walk on water. But if you think he had anything to do with DeRocher's fraudulent MS research, you're way off base."

"Honey," he said gently. "I have proof."

Eight

Jill stared at Hunter in disbelief, her mind spinning as she tried to figure out what he could possibly have found out. Or was he just bluffing? she wondered. Using that journalistic tactician's mind of his to trap her into admitting what *she* knew? "What kind of proof?" she finally hedged.

"Copies of memos from Neals to DeRocher in which he's giving permission to, as he refers to it, 'hasten the reporting process.' In other words, report things that hadn't even happened yet. Then there are computer log reports that show that Neals logged on huge amounts of computer time in the week prior to the first press release. A copy of a report mentioning the so-called MS breakthrough that he sent to the Board, dated three days *before* DeRocher supposedly told him about it. Neals was telling the Ackertons about something that, according to later reports. he didn't even know about yet."

"I don't believe a word of it!" Jill felt stiff with shock. "Somebody's just trying to discredit Dr. Neals. Or to throw suspicion onto him and away from themselves."

"Like they did with you?"

There wasn't a lot she could say to that, so Jill simply looked at him in silence.

"You were set up by your old prof, honey."

"If you really believe that, why haven't you used it in your articles?" Her heart was thumping so loudly she wondered if Hunter could hear it. It was impossible! There was no way Dr. Neals had been involved. Hunter was just casting bait to see what came to the surface.

"Because I'm scared to death, that's why," he told her forcefully. "Scared that he's got you in some hold I don't know about, scared that if I start stirring up that hornet's nest again without knowing exactly what the hell's going on, I'll get you hurt worse than you're hurting now." He reached out to touch her cheek. "I wish you could tell me what's really going on, Jill. I wish you trusted me enough to make me a part of whatever's happening."

"I wish I could tell you, too," Jill whispered, suddenly aching with a bone-deep emptiness. She stepped toward him instinctively and he folded his arms around her, warming her. She shivered and nestled nearer to him, closing her eyes.

"But you won't."

"I can't."

"Jill—" He stopped abruptly. Then he kissed the top of her head and pushed her gently away from him. "You'd better get to work before Douglass sends out the National Guard."

She nodded, finding it hard to meet his eyes. "Will I see you . . . tonight?"

Hunter placed a knuckle under her chin and tipped her face up, grinning lazily. "All of me," he purred, his eyes holding hers warmly. "All night."

Jill had to smile. "Shrimp en brochette and pilaf, my place, about seven? I'll leave my extra key with the manager and if I'm late, let yourself in and make yourself a drink."

Hunter's grin widened. "I kind of liked that pizza last night."

"I think you kind of liked the fact we ate it in bed, and as I remember it, we didn't even finish because you got sidetracked."

Hunter's laugh was hearty. "How can a man not get sidetracked when he's in bed with a gorgeous, naked woman? I thought the fact we polished off most of the pizza before making love said a lot about my willpower."

"Even if you did drip cheese all over my—"

"—and licked it off," Hunter reminded her throatily. "Honey, if we keep this conversation going much longer, Douglass isn't going to see you at all today."

Jill pulled open the glass door to the living room, pausing to blow him a kiss. "See you at seven."

"How about a romantic walk on the beach to watch the sunset first? I'll pick you up at the lab when you're through."

"Sounds nice, but Brett and I are heading down to Naples all day to check out a reported panther sighting. I probably won't get back before six or so."

Hunter's brows pulled together. "You tell Douglass that if he lets any of his local wildlife lay claw on you, he'd better give up any plans he has of fathering children."

Jill slipped through the open door, giving Hunter a wide smile. "You'll be glad to hear he feels the same way about you. One word from me, and you'll be 'gator bait." She slid the door closed on his pungent reply, still laughing as she let herself out of his apartment.

But as she made her way out to where she'd parked her car the previous night, her smile turned to a frown. Sooner or later she was going to have a serious talk with Hunter about Phoenix. He'd been right this morning when he'd said they couldn't carry it into marriage. She unlocked the car door and slid into the driver's seat, wrinkling her nose at the heat. She started the engine and turned the air-conditioning up high, feeling the sweat trickle along her hairline as she sat there for a minute or two. Seven months ago, she'd run away from Hunter for exactly that reason: because she couldn't tell him what was going on and couldn't afford to have him snooping around. And here she was going through the same nightmare again. What had Hunter said this morning? Déjà vu.

Maybe tonight, she debated as she wheeled the car out of the guests' parking lot. She'd cook shrimp on the outside grill, serve him a good wine, and then gently and delicately go over everything that had happened. And somehow, she had to convince him never to reveal a word of it to anyone.

He was going to have to tell her. Hunter dropped back into the wicker chair after Jill had left and sipped his lukewarm coffee, staring out across the water. The beach was dotted with shell hunters and birds, and a small boat moved slowly just offshore, nearly becalmed in the light breeze. Hunter watched without really seeing it.

Sooner or later, he was going to have to tell Jill everything. His investigations at Phoenix had taken him in circles until just a couple of weeks ago when something had fallen into place. He still wasn't certain what he had, or even where it fit, but there was definitely a link; he could feel it all the way to his bones. And all because he'd spent three weeks in California interviewing the science and medical faculty at Berkeley and had decided, purely on the spur of the moment, to spend a couple of days in Las Vegas trying his hand at the blackjack tables.

He wouldn't have even noticed the man had he not been at the center of a huge crowd at one of the roulette wheels. Curious, Hunter had worked his way nearer the table to discover Dr. Preston Neals sitting there, pale and disheveled and glassy-eyed. There was a glass of what looked like neat bourbon beside him, and he looked as though he hadn't eaten or slept in days. He had a huge stack of high-money chips in front of him and at every spin of the wheel he leaned forward raptly, nearly trembling with excitement.

Hunter had stayed for only a minute or two and then had turned away, sickened. He'd seen that look on men's faces before, and knew what it meant. Dr. Preston Neals, the most brilliant mind in biochemistry in the world today, was a gambling fool.

He'd wandered over to the blackjack tables and had played for a while, quitting when he'd tripled his original wager. By that time the crowd around Neals had thinned and he'd strolled back to the roulette wheel. Neals was still there, but the stack of chips in front of him had shrunk to three and he looked sick. He'd taken a long swallow of bourbon just then and by chance his gaze had met Hunter's. He'd paused, growing puzzled as he tried to recall where he'd seen that face before. Then he'd remembered.

He'd flung the glass away from him with a bellow and had exploded to his feet, screaming obscenities and trying to crawl across the table toward Hunter with a look of such vitriolic hatred on his face that the handful of people watching had fallen back in shock. Two large security men had appeared instantly and had tried to quiet him with a minimum of fuss, but Neals had no intention of being silenced. He'd started screaming threats at Hunter, accusing him of having jinxed his luck at the table, of ruining his career, of destroying his life. He'd gone a little crazy, his face mottled with rage as he'd clawed and fought with the two security men, trying to get at Hunter. They'd called in reinforcements and a minute or two later Neals had been swiftly escorted from the casino, still screaming incoherently.

Apologies had been made, feathers smoothed. A young, well dressed casino manager had handed Hunter a roll of complimentary chips and a glass of very old Scotch along with another apology, and it hadn't taken Hunter very long to find out that Neals was a regular at the tables. Although, the young manager had assured him, he'd never gone berserk before, even when losing heavily. "Does he lose often?" Hunter had asked cautiously. The young manager had smiled then, a predatory, sharklike smile totally at odds with his clean-cut prep school image. "Very often," he replied. And during the next hour, Hunter had discovered just how heavily Preston Neals lost, and how much he owed.

Where the information left him, Hunter had no idea. But it was a clue. And it had something to do with Phoenix. Neals was still at Phoenix, as were Simon DeRocher, John Conyers and one other of the original six-person team. The other two had been sacrificed along with Jill. Including Poul Wilczek, Hunter recalled suddenly. And Jill thought Wilczek had been working with DeRocher to create the fraudulent research material. He took another sip of cold coffee, eyes narrowed as he tried to fit the pieces together. Wilczek might be a lead he hadn't followed far enough. If he *had* been in the original plan, he'd have been plenty upset to find himself being tossed to the sharks while DeRocher and

Conyers stayed clean. Upset enough to talk, maybe. Hunter smiled.

And Neals? Hunter got to his feet and started gathering up the dishes, his smile widening. Neals was the weak link in the whole thing, and Neals was where it was all going to start coming apart.

It was nearly eight-thirty by the time Jill had finally inched her way to the end of the Sanibel-Fort Meyers causeway in the heavy tourist traffic, and after nine before she turned her small car into her parking spot at the Sea's Glory condos. She gave the guest parking lot a glance on the way by and smiled when she saw Hunter's rental sitting with its hood under a coconut palm. Typical Yankee, she thought fondly as she hurried up to the apartment. It usually took one good dent in the hood for most northern visitors to Florida to realize that parking under coconut palms was not a great idea. As she waited for the elevator, juggling two bags of groceries, she laughed at herself. She'd been one of those Boston Yankees herself not long ago. It was going to be hard to go back to falling leaves and crisp mornings.

Back? The elevator's door whispered open, and Jill stepped inside, frowning. Back to what? To where? She had no past to go back to. All that existed for her now was the future, and it was going to be whatever she made of it. Thanks to Simon DeRocher, and his greed for immortality.

Jill's mouth tightened and she felt tendrils of hot, bright anger weave through her at the mere thought of the name. Clever Simon, Roberta Wu had called him, not even bothering to hide her dislike—or her distrust. "Watch that guy," she'd told Jill a week or two after Jill had joined Phoenix. "He's as ambitious as they come, and he's not the type to let a little thing like fair play or loyalty come between him and what he wants." You should have listened to her, Jill told herself. You could have saved yourself and everyone else a lot of grief if you'd gone to Dr. Neals with your suspicions right at the beginning.

But she hadn't. Part of it had been simple professional loyalty toward a colleague, and part of it was the self-admitted knowledge that she wasn't the easiest person to work with, either. None of them was. At any one time, there were as many as forty scientists working at Phoenix, broken up into teams of five or six, and personality conflicts were inevitable. They were all very good at what they did, and the natural self-assurance and impatience that goes with being the best man made them difficult to work with. At Phoenix, all those idiosyncrasies that made them temperamentally unsuited for teamwork were humored. That's where they'd gone wrong with Simon. Because in Simon, self-assurance had evolved into arrogance and contempt, the drive to discover corrupted into the drive to be discovered. Nobel Fever at its worst.

That hadn't made going to Neals with her complaints and suspicions any easier, though, for the simple reason that she'd been afraid that her feelings were caused partially by jealousy. She'd been one of Neals's favorites once. He'd encouraged her, had helped her career by putting the right words in the right ears and had always urged her to go as far as she could. When she'd joined Phoenix, she'd thought things would be the same as they'd been when she'd worked with him at Stanford. But it hadn't been like that. He'd been friendly, even warm, toward her; but it was obvious that Simon DeRocher had supplanted her as Neals's next young up-and-coming favorite.

She'd heard a lot about DeRocher before coming to Phoenix. Two years her junior, he'd come up through the field like a blazing comet, leaving Stanford to work in England before joining Phoenix. But Jill had quickly discovered that the man didn't live up to the reputation, and they'd clashed almost immediately. At first Jill had put De-Rocher's antagonism down to his own jealousy of the special relationship she still shared with Neals. Later she realized it was simple fear—fear that Jill would see through the sleight of hand and expose him for the moderately competent scientist he was. The fact that she couldn't be bluffed as he'd bluffed so many made her dangerous, and Jill now realized she was lucky to come out of the Phoenix madness as relatively unharmed as she had.

If being tossed out of the profession in disgrace and knowing that your associates and friends thought of you as a cheat, a liar and a fraud could be called unharmed, Jill reminded herself with a humorless smile. The elevator bell chimed and she waited for the doors to open. If knowing that you'd never work again at what you loved, and that all the work you'd done for nearly ten years had been for nothing, could be called lucky. And, all the while, knowing that Simon DeRocher was still out there, unscathed by the evil he'd perpetrated.

In spite of herself, Jill had to smile as she walked down to her apartment. Not quite unscathed, she reminded herself with satisfaction. "I got the last word, Clever Simon," she whispered, pushing the door open. "You might cheat your way to that Nobel yet, but you're sure as hell not going to do it on *my* work!"

To Jill's surprise, the apartment was dark and silent. Not bothering to turn on the foyer light, she kicked her mud-stained sneakers off and walked toward the kitchen. Reflections from the pool lights danced off the ceiling and walls of the living room and she stopped as she walked by the door, frowning slightly. The faint scent of cigarette smoke caught her attention, movement where there should have been none. Her heart gave a thump and she stared into the spangled darkness. "Hunter, is that you?"

There was the sound of someone shifting heavily, the clink of ice on glass. "Yeah." Hunter's voice was like sandpaper.

Jill felt a jolt of relief and laughed, continuing on to the kitchen. "Sorry I'm so late," she called back to him. "I think two-thirds of the population of Florida is taking an early weekend. Between accidents and nervous drivers the highway was jammed and the causeway was a disaster."

She set the two bags down onto the counter and started unpacking them. "I thought we'd save the shrimp for tomorrow night and settle for steak and salad tonight, that okay?" There was no answer and Jill paused, then shrugged and started unpacking the second bag. "Or we can go out, although I'll need to shower and change."

There was no reply. Jill frowned slightly, then pulled open the carton of ice cream she was holding, dug a spoon out of the drawer and scooped up a generous mound of fudge nut ripple. She gave it a lick as she walked into the living room. "Why are you sitting in the dark?"

She switched on one of the low table lamps. Hunter grunted and shielded his eyes. He was sitting on the brocade sofa in front of the window, elbows on knees, an open bottle of Scotch and a half-filled glass on the table in front of him. A cigarette dangled from one hand and he took a deep drag, easing the smoke out in a thin stream.

"I thought you'd quit," she said in honest surprise.

"I did." His voice was no more than a growl.

Jill walked around the coffee table and sat on the sofa beside him, one foot tucked under her. She held out the spoonful of ice cream. "It's your favorite."

Hunter looked at the spoon, eyes squinted against the light, then shook his head. Jill looked at it herself, perplexed, then set it on a newspaper lying on the table. She brushed a tangle of toast-brown hair off Hunter's forehead and leaned forward to kiss him. "Bad day?"

"Yeah."

He made no move to kiss her back, and Jill could have sworn he pulled away slightly at her touch. She looked at him thoughtfully, then at the bottle of Scotch. It was down by a good fourth. "I thought you'd given that up, too," she said quietly.

He did look at her then, his gaze holding hers with an indefinable expression. He took a deep breath and flexed his shoulders as though they ached, then leaned across and ground the cigarette into an ashtray. "It helps, some days."

"And today?"

"Not even close."

His voice was hoarse, and she glanced at the open cigarette package lying beside him. It was nearly empty. "Hunter, what's—?"

"There's something I've got to tell you, Jill." He stared at the glass of Scotch as though wondering if he wanted it or not, and Jill felt a cold finger run down her spine. "It's there." He nodded toward the newspaper. "On the front page."

Jill looked at the paper for the first time. It was a copy of the *Miami Herald* and she reached down and pulled it toward her curiously. There was a blurred photograph on the front page, and it took her a moment or two to realize that it was Dr. Preston Neals smiling broadly up at her. She recognized the picture. It had been taken the day that he and Dean Ackerton had announced that a team of research biochemists at Phoenix had discovered a cure for multiple sclerosis.

The later editions of all the newspapers carrying the original story had revised their headlines to explain that the

Phoenix team had made a major medical breakthrough and were on the *verge* of discovering a cure. But by that time, in most people's minds and most importantly in the minds of the Board of Directors at Ackerton Pharmaceutical, the distinction between actually having found a cure and merely being on the verge of finding it had blurred. Hands had been shaken, congratulations given, massive additional funding approved, and Team Four of Phoenix Research had gone down in history. Eight days later, they were in the headlines again, but this time for a radically different reason. And the picture showing up on the front pages then was of a stunned, dark-eyed woman named Jill Benedict.

It had been about then that Jill had stopped reading newspapers. "What's going on?"

"He's dead, Jill." Hunter's voice was soft. "He killed himself."

Time stopped. In the stillness, Jill could hear the ice cubes in Hunter's drink crackling, a faint burst of laughter from someone out by the pool. She shivered suddenly, feeling strangely apart from this room, from Hunter. "What—" Her voice cracked and she swallowed. "What do you mean?"

Hunter put his arm around her shoulders and rubbed her bare arm. "I heard it in a news bulletin about noon and have been trying to get you ever since. Kathy called Naples, but they weren't able to get you on the truck radio."

"We—we were out in the swamp," Jill whispered, reaching out to draw the paper nearer. Her hand seemed to move very slowly, as though in a dream. "We found clear signs of a panther, female we think. Maybe even kittens...." She realized she was talking nonsense and let the sentence fade off, still staring at Neals's picture. "How? What happened?"

Hunter was silent for a long while. "His wife found him about nine this morning. He'd been eating breakfast when he just got up from the table and walked out of the house without saying anything. His wife said she didn't think anything of it, that when he got preoccupied about something at work he sometimes wandered around in a fog for days." He was quiet again for a minute or two, as though giving her an opportunity to absorb what he'd told her so far. "She figured he'd gone to work. She was going out to visit friends, and when she went out to get her car, she found his still there." The pressure of his arm tightened. "He'd shot himself."

"Oh, my God." Jill stared at the picture, her mind spinning, unable to comprehend what he was saying. "Why?" she whispered. "Why would he do that?" But even as she said the words, she knew. "Simon DeRocher." She turned her head to look at Hunter. "DeRocher killed him, Hunter."

Hunter looked startled. Then he shook his head slowly, his face grim. "Nobody killed him, Jill. He did it himself. He left a note, apparently."

But Jill shook her head firmly. "Hunter, I mean it. Simon had information about Dr. Neals and was blackmailing him into keeping quiet about the MS project. But it must have gotten to be too much, first the Apocalypse Project, then the Phoenix scandal. Simon DeRocher killed Dr. Neals as certainly as if he'd pulled the trigger himself."

Hunter's expression went even grimmer. "Jill, if anyone was responsible for Preston Neals's death, it was me."

This time, Jill looked startled. "You? You mean for exposing the Phoenix fraud?"

A muscle tickled in Hunter's jaw and he drew his arm from around her. He rested his forearms on his thighs and leaned on them heavily, letting his hands hang limply between his knees. He stared at the carpet between his feet. "Jill, I've been all over Neals for the past three months. Ever since I made up my mind to get to the bottom of what happened at Phoenix. I knew he was in on it somehow, that he and DeRocher had stuck together while you took the heat." He looked up at her, his rugged face hollowed in the dim light. "I went to see him about nine weeks ago and told him I was out to get him, that I wasn't going to quit until he—and DeRocher—paid for what they did to you." He looked back down at the carpet. "I knew he'd crack sooner or later. But I had no idea . . ."

"My God," Jill whispered, feeling sick. She closed her eyes. "Oh, Hunter, how could you? You had no idea what was going on, no idea at all."

"I was trying to find *out* what happened, remember?" Hunter's voice was testy. Then he rubbed his stubbled cheeks with his hands wearily, sighing, and reached for the glass. He finished the Scotch in one long swallow.

"Oh, damn it, Hunter, why couldn't you just let it go!" Jill picked up the newspaper and flung it across the room, sending the spoon and a blob of melted ice cream flying. She stood up violently. "Everything was under control. I should have known you'd never just drop the thing when you were supposed to. You're like a damned juggernaut—point you in the right direction and give you a push, and you just plow down anything that gets in your way."

Hunter was staring at her. "What do you mean, everything was under control?"

"I mean you were supposed to expose the rot at Phoenix, not turn this thing into a personal crusade! It never occurred to me that you'd—" She stopped abruptly. Then she gazed down at him, her anger gentling. "That you'd fall in love with me," she said softly. "That you'd get a sudden urge to be all heroic and go charging around the woods trying to save your lady from the dragons she'd put there herself.'' She smiled faintly. "You're such a chivalrous idiot at times, Kincaide. I guess that's where I went wrong. I forgot that under that liberated exterior beats the heart of an old-fashioned man, one who wouldn't let his woman fight her own fights.''

"What the *hell* are you talking about?'' Hunter rumbled, obviously not understanding a thing she was saying but not liking the direction it seemed to be heading.

She gazed back at him wonderingly. "You really didn't know, did you?''

"All I know is that you're talking in circles, lady!''

She laughed. "You were my secret weapon, Kincaide. My instrument of revenge. Except,'' she added quietly, with a glance at the scattered newspaper, "I lost control at the end.''

"Jill,'' Hunter said with quiet threat.

"Didn't you ever think it was odd that you never found out who called you that afternoon at Chapel Hill, telling you that the Phoenix announcement was a hoax? Or who kept you supplied with all those anonymous tips during the next week, making sure you were on the right trail?''

Hunter's eyes narrowed as he pieced together what she was saying. He got to his feet slowly. "Are you telling me that it was *you*?''

She blinked, suddenly uncertain as he moved around the end of the coffee table toward her. "Partly,'' she admitted, edging backward a step or two. "I got a grad student at Duke University to actually make the calls. I paid him a hundred bucks to keep him quiet and promised him a job recommendation after he gets his degree.'' She smiled bitterly. "Which is pretty worthless now, I guess. The only thing a recommendation from me will get him is slammed doors.''

"I don't believe this," Hunter said conversationally. "Are you saying that the whole time we were together in Chapel Hill, the whole time I was investigating Phoenix, you were feeding me information?"

She swallowed, looked away. Then she nodded. "I guess I should start from the top."

"That," said Hunter with deadly calm, "might be an idea."

Jill glanced up at him uncertainly. She'd prayed the day would never come when she'd have to tell him all this, yet now it was here she could see it had simply been a matter of time. In a way she was glad. She walked across to the sofa and sat down. "I don't know where to start," she said helplessly, daring to look up at him again.

He was staring down at her, face intent. "You said it, lady. Start at the top."

She sighed. He wasn't going to make it easy. Which was hardly surprising, all things considered. She took another deep breath, then looked up at him. "The Phoenix hoax was all Simon's idea. He was blackmailing both me and Dr. Neals into keeping quiet about it."

"Blackmailing you over what?" Hunter sounded annoyed now. "Remember I investigated that Phoenix mess inside out, Jill. And that included investigating you, before we . . . got to know each other better. You're as clean as new snow. The only thing anyone could blackmail you for is a terminal case of nice."

"It wasn't me. It was Dr. Neals." She stopped, rubbing at a grass stain on the knee of her jeans. "Have you ever heard of the Apocalypse Project?" Hunter gave a negative grunt. "It was a government project back in the early fifties, run out of a lab in Iowa somewhere. The facility's been closed for years."

"Radiation tests?"

"Chemicals. Biological warfare. That sort of thing."

"Nice people."

Jill shrugged. "It was just after the war, remember, and before the Geneva Convention."

"And Neals worked there."

"He headed up the Apocalypse Project. I don't know the details, but it had to do with an exceptionally viral form of anthrax." Hunter's startled oath was earthy. "There was an accident, and three people were infected before the contamination could be contained. They all died. Horribly." Jill glanced at Hunter. He was staring at her in fascination, and she had to smile. "We don't do things like that anymore, Hunt."

"Tell that to the sheep that died in Montana and southern Alberta a few years ago."

"Well, *I* don't do anything like that," she clarified a bit testily. It was a sore point with her that germ warfare was the first thing people thought of when they heard the word *biochemist*. "Anyway, Neals was to blame for the toxic release. He was overworked and exhausted, and he forgot to close the inner containment vessel. One of the men who died was his best friend, a bacteriologist by the name of Carl Oftag. Oftag had been working on a secondary project before the accident, developing pure strains of viruses in the lab."

She glanced up at Hunter and realized she'd lost him. "As early as 1931, they knew that some forty diseases, including smallpox, rabies and polio, were caused by viruses, but they didn't know anything about the actual viruses themselves. In order to study them, you need to grow and observe them under controlled conditions. It wasn't until the late forties, and antibiotics, that scientists could grow them successfully. Once they had samples of viruses, they could run experiments on them and determine what killed them."

She saw understanding dawn, and nodded. "That's right. Vaccines. The fact that Oftag was looking for vaccines to protect military personnel while they dumped deadly viruses on the enemy doesn't lessen the impact of the work. By 1955, four years after the Apocalypse accident, Dr. Preston Neals's work in this field had led to the development of vaccines for three major diseases, including polio. From there he went into immunology, and you know all about his work on organ transplants. All of today's heart transplants have Dr. Neals to thank."

Hunter whistled. Then, suddenly, his eyes narrowed. "Wait a minute. If Oftag died four years earlier, how did Neals—?" Jill didn't say anything, letting him think it through. After a moment he gave another long, low whistle. "He stole Oftag's work!"

Nine

Stole is a strong word," Jill protested quietly. "When Dr. Neals was going through Oftag's personal effects, he found all his research notes. He realized how important they were, and he also knew that Oftag's work would probably be lost to medical science unless he . . . did something with it."

Hunter gave a derisive snort and Jill rubbed at the grass stain again. "It was wrong, and Dr. Neals knew it. He hadn't intended to take the credit himself, but one breakthrough followed another and somehow, in all the excitement, he just . . . never got around to admitting he hadn't done the advance work himself." She looked up. "Hunter, he wasn't an evil man. He was just weak. An opportunity fell into his lap, and he grabbed it. I know it was unethical, but—"

"Unethical, my—" Hunter caught himself. "He stole the work from a dead man, Jill. He built his career and reputation on a lie. Hell, the man was even nominated for a

Nobel a few years ago for that drug he came up with that suppresses the body's immune system so it won't reject transplanted organs. A nomination that should have been Carl Oftag's!'' He strode around the room angrily. "How long have you known about this?"

His voice held an undercurrent of accusation, and Jill looked at him sharply. "DeRocher told me seven months ago, after I threatened to go to the Ethics Review Committee with his so-called MS find. He told me that if I told anyone that he and Conyers had messed around with the test data, he'd expose the whole story about Neals. He kept Dr. Neals quiet with the same threat."

"And you went along with it?" Hunter's voice lifted on disbelief. "The man was a bigger fraud than DeRocher, Jill!"

"The man is—was—a brilliant biochemist. He repaid society a thousand times over for that mistake, Hunter."

"Oh, come off it, Jill! Neals didn't make a 'mistake,' he stole another scientist's work and pretended it was his own. Just because he went on to develop drugs that have helped thousands doesn't make it any better. You can't wipe out past sins with good deeds."

"Dr. Neals did not steal—" Jill caught her anger, biting it back. "You cannot pretend that thirty years of brilliant work don't exist just because of that one wrong. Don't try to tell me you've never done anything you're ashamed of, Kincaide!"

"I've done plenty I'm ashamed of," he grated, "but I didn't go on to build an entire career out of lies."

"No?" Jill's anger blazed. "I'd say you've come pretty close. Most of what you write is about lies—other peoples' lies and mistakes. You never write about the good in peoples' lives."

"Maybe because there's precious little of it," Hunter shot back. He fought visibly to get his temper under control. "And that's why you kept quiet about DeRocher's little games? To protect Neals?" Jill glared at him, then the anger dissipated and she nodded. Hunter swore in an undertone, still pacing. "Then you brought me into it."

Again, it was full of accusation and anger. Jill sighed. "I couldn't expose DeRocher's fraud, but I was damned if I was going to let him get away with it. I figured that if the press got hold of a rumor that there hadn't been a breakthrough at all, the truth would come out sooner or later."

"So you used me."

"Hunter, you were the only weapon I had, don't you see that?" She looked up at him pleadingly. "I'd read your stories on political corruption, and that series you did on government involvement in Central America. I knew it was your kind of story, full of greed and fabrication. I knew that once Bulldog Kincaide got his teeth in the story, you'd never let go until you'd uncovered the whole mess."

"But you didn't count on DeRocher swinging the guilt around onto you."

"I knew there was a chance he'd try. I never underestimated DeRocher, Hunter. That's why I chose you, because you were strong enough and smart enough to catch him. And I just didn't know what else to do."

He stared down at her almost admiringly, then gave a snort of laughter. "I'll be damned," he murmured, shaking his head. "All this time I've been tearing myself apart with guilt for blundering in and stirring up the hornet's nest that got you stung, and in fact you were orchestrating the whole thing."

Jill looked away uncomfortably. "I'm sorry," she whispered. "I should have told you. But I was afraid that if you knew there was a possibility that I'd wind up taking the blame for the whole mess, you wouldn't go through with it."

"I wouldn't have," he said bluntly. "It stinks, Jill. You take the blame, Neals's dirty little secret stays safe, and DeRocher walks away without so much as a scratch."

Jill didn't bother answering, and Hunter muttered something under his breath she was glad she didn't hear. "I don't understand how you could let him get away with it," he said in exasperation. "Everyone thinks DeRocher did most of the MS work at Phoenix and was well on his way to a cure when you invalidated the tests—instead of the other way around. Your career is ruined, and DeRocher is going to come out of this a legend. He's going to build up his career on work he stole from you, just like Neals did with Oftag."

"Not quite."

Hunter stopped his pacing. He looked down at her, eyes narrowing. "You did something, didn't you?"

Jill smiled dryly. "I'm not quite as gullible as you think I am, Kincaide. Of course I did something." The impatience on his face vanished under curiosity, and Jill laughed softly. "I may suffer from 'terminal nice,' Hunter, but I don't like being crossed any more than you do. After your first article on suspected fraud at Phoenix hit the stands, the Board hit the roof. They ordered all work on the MS project stopped, then—on the off chance that you were on to something and not just setting yourself up for a lawsuit—they had the lab sealed to prevent anyone from covering his tracks. When they discovered that the data *had* been played around with, they brought the Ethics people in. The rest you know: The evidence pointed to me. They put a security guard at the door of my office so I couldn't clear out any incriminating evidence, confiscated all my research notes and material, then escorted me off the premises until a full hearing could be held."

She gave her head a toss, still remembering her stunned disbelief at finding her own office off-limits, of walking down that long corridor to the door of Phoenix with two burly security guards beside her. Remembering, too, the shock and horror in the eyes of her fellow scientists as they'd watched silently, most unable to even meet her eyes as she walked by. "Thanks to Dr. Neals, I had a three hour warning. So I used it." She smiled coldly at the memory. "I snuck into my lab, tossed most of my handwritten notes into the nearest shredder, then logged onto the lab computer and took a page out of DeRocher's own book and changed a few numbers here and there."

Hunter's brows pulled together. "What do you mean?"

"All my research material—the material DeRocher is now using—is next to worthless. He'll never be able to duplicate our test results in a million years. I didn't do anything too obvious because I didn't want to make him suspicious, but I changed enough to throw everything off. And he's not good enough to figure out what went wrong." Her smile turned a bit malicious. "If he becomes a legend in his own time, he'll have to do it on *his* work, not mine."

Hunter stared at her. Then, as the impact of what she said sunk in fully, he gave a whoop of delighted laughter. "I always took you as too sweet and forgiving for your own good, but I'm beginning to believe you're about as sweet and forgiving as that 'gator you were playing with yesterday."

Jill smiled with real warmth. "I have my moments, Kincaide."

"But there's something I still don't understand," he said softly. "Why did you run away? I figured it was because you blamed me for everything that happened at Phoenix, but if you *planned* the story to break . . ."

"I ran because I was terrified," Jill said simply.

"Of me?" The question was torn out of him.

"Of you. Of myself. You, because you'd turned into someone I didn't know anymore. You kept pushing and pushing, putting everything, even me, second to that damned story. And I was afraid of myself because I wanted you so badly." She smiled faintly at the expression on his face. "You were using me, Hunt, and I didn't even care, isn't that wild? I knew you wanted the story, and I was ready to give it to you. I was tempted to tell you everything just to please you. I hated how vulnerable I'd become. I was terrified you'd find out about Neals, either on your own or because I'd finally just tell you, so I panicked and ran. I thought if I disappeared, you'd figure the story was finished and forget all about Neals and Phoenix." She smiled again. "But you didn't. True to your nickname, you wouldn't let go once you'd tasted blood."

"Neals." He made the name sound like something obscene. "You did all that just to protect Neals."

"I had to." Jill sighed, knowing he'd never understand. "I'm a good biochemist, Hunter. Very good, as a matter of fact. But I didn't get that way all by myself. Dr. Neals saw a special spark in me way back when I was in college, and he took me under his wing. The man was more generous with his time and knowledge than I could repay in a hundred years. I'm twenty-seven years old, I spent a year working at the top research facility in the entire world, with scientists who are literally the cream of the crop, and I was inches away from pinning down a cure for some of the most horrifying diseases known to man. I've already passed on all my research material to a friend at the National Institutes of Health at Bethesda. He'll finish what I started. The fact that I'll never be credited with it doesn't matter, Hunter. What matters is that *I* know I did it. Now, how many people get to do something they'd dreamed about?'' She gazed up at him. ''I *owe* Neals this, don't you see that?''

Hunter stared down at her, wishing, not for the first time in the last couple of days, that he'd stayed in Washington. Planting his hands on his hips he shook his head and swore between his teeth. He stared at the carpet for a silent moment. There was no way to tell her this but straight out, he realized. Although, after hearing all he'd just heard, it was going to be like slapping her across the face. *Forgive me, Jill,* he silently asked her.

''I thought that when I finally had proof that I was right, I was going to enjoy rubbing your stubborn little nose in it and saying 'I told you so.' Instead, I almost wish I'd been wrong.'' His eyes met hers. They were troubled now, wary of more hurt. ''But I *was* right, Jill. You were used. Neals knew exactly what DeRocher was up to, in fact he gave him the idea in the first place. And when it started to fall apart, when they had to come up with something real fast to save their skins, they used you as the sacrificial lamb.''

Impatience flickered in her eyes. ''I don't believe that.''

''Will you believe it if Neals tells you himself?'' Hunter snapped. He immediately regretted his impatience, recognizing his anger was at Neals's duplicity, not at Jill. He swore again, with considerable feeling, and walked across to where he'd tossed his jacket earlier. He took the large envelope from the inner pocket and walked back to Jill, unfolding the envelope and slipping the papers from it as he sat beside her. ''You're not going to like this,'' he told her gruffly. ''I got it about two this afternoon, and I've been sitting here all day trying to decide whether to give it to you or not. But you're going to find out sooner or later, and it may as well be now, from me.''

Jill looked at the papers, then at him. Her eyes were wide and frightened, and Hunter wished he had Preston Neals's throat in his hands instead of this letter. She looked back at the papers and swallowed. "What is it?"

"Read it, Jill," Hunter said gently, placing the papers in her lap. She held her hands tightly clenched, as though by not taking the letter she could deny its existence. *She knows,* he suddenly realized, his heart aching for her. *She's suspected all along; she just hasn't let herself believe it. But she knows.*

Slowly, as though mesmerized, Jill started reading the first page. Hunter already knew it by heart. "Dear Mr. Kincaide," it started. "By now you know..."

Hunter stood up and walked across to a glass-and-black-lacquer tea cart set diagonally across one corner of the room. There was a formidable array of decanters and liquor bottles on the mirrored top, and glasses stacked beneath. He picked up one of the glasses and walked back to where Jill was sitting, then sat beside her again and poured her a generous shot of Scotch. He set the glass on the table in front of her, saying nothing. He heard her breath catch and looked at her, tracing her profile with his eyes. Something glittered on her cheek and she reached up and wiped the tears away, her hand trembling. She took another sobbing breath and Hunter looked away, his teeth aching from gritting them so hard.

The minutes passed. Silence enfolded the room, except for Jill's occasional shaky indrawn breath and the ticking of a distant clock. Hunter looked at the bottle of Scotch in front of him contemplatively, then screwed the cap on firmly and set it aside. Liquid oblivion was a little too tempting tonight, he brooded, staring into the glass. In a hundred hellholes the world round, he'd watched too many men lose themselves that way, preferring the dreamless oblivion of the bottle to the nightmare of reality. It was a waste of good talent and good lives, and he'd sworn he'd never let it catch him. But there were some nights, he thought savagely, when it was damn tempting.

"I don't understand."

It took him a moment to realize Jill had spoken. Hunter looked at her, wincing inwardly when her tear-glazed eyes met his, filled with desperate bewilderment. He picked up the glass of liquor and put it in her hand. "Drink that."

"I hate Scotch," she whispered.

"Drink it anyway."

To Hunter's surprise, she took a sip, making a face as she forced herself to swallow it. But she took another sip, blinking as her eyes started to water, then shuddered and put the glass down. It wouldn't dull the pain, he decided, but it might stop the shivers that had been racking her for the past five minutes. "He needed the bonus money Ackerton was promising," he said after a few minutes of silence. Jill was staring down at the papers in her hand, but he doubted she was seeing them.

"What do you mean?" she said faintly.

"He was a gambler. I don't mean he bought the occasional lottery ticket or played poker once a week. I mean he was into some very heavy gambling, with some very heavy Las Vegas types. The types who don't like it when you can't pay your debts."

"Dr. Neals?" She looked at him, her eyes dark and hurt. They grew puzzled. She shook her head slowly. "I don't believe that. Dr. Neals wouldn't even let us run a football pool at Phoenix. And I remember at Stanford he nearly fired one of the lab techs when he found out she went to the races occasionally."

"Because he recognized the disease in himself, and knew how vulnerable it makes people—to greed, or blackmail."

"I don't believe it."

"Jill," Hunter said quietly. "I saw him at Las Vegas. He was so far gone he wasn't even touching reality anymore. I asked around, he was well-known out there."

"But . . ." He watched her fight it, trying to understand, to put the pieces in some sort of order that she could understand. "I still don't understand how he could have done it," she whispered. "I *trusted* him."

"That's what he and DeRocher counted on. They knew you'd believe anything Neals told you. It didn't take much to convince DeRocher to do it, of course. Conyers simply did as he was told. They'd already anticipated that you'd give them trouble—I suspect by that time Neals was regretting ever having brought you to Phoenix. By then, DeRocher had found out about the Apocalypse Project and Oftag's death, and when Neals got cold feet about implicating you, DeRocher used the knowledge to keep him quiet." Hunter took a swallow of Jill's Scotch, letting it warm him before he went on. "I doubt it took much convincing. As you said, Neals was weak and easily led. He'd probably suggested the fraud to DeRocher on a desperate whim, frantic for money, then regretted it. Once DeRocher took over, Neals could convince himself that he didn't have any choice but go along with it." He turned his head sideways to look at her. "Jill, I'm sorry. I know how you felt about the man."

And I know how badly you're hurting, too, he brooded. The shock, the hurt, the betrayal. Neals had used her. Terrified, he'd panicked and flung the nearest sacrificial victim to the lions, hoping to placate them. The fact that it had been Jill hadn't mattered; it was doubtful, in those last few days, that he even realized the enormity of what he and DeRocher had done. Only afterward, reading the newspapers and listening to people talk, would he gradually begin to understand what he'd done to her. In saving his life, he'd destroyed hers. And not even a weak and fearful man like Preston Neals could live with that guilt forever. Not if he had a spark of caring left in him.

Jill picked up her drink, looked at it for a long moment, then put it down again, untouched.

"Are you all right?"

She nodded slowly, looking a little shell-shocked. "I guess so," she whispered. "You were right all along. When you started investigating Neals seven months ago, I thought you were crazy. I was terrified you'd find out about the Apocalypse Project, but I just never dreamed that...that he was involved with the mess at Phoenix."

Hunter reached out and brushed a stray tear from her cheek. "Put it down to chronic cynicism. I've spent years uncovering people's unpleasant little secrets, and I've discovered no one's immune from stupidity and greed." He smiled and tipped her chin up with his knuckle. "Or from too much trust."

"Oh, God, I wish this were all over!" she exclaimed with a shudder. She covered her face with her hands, then swept her fingers through her hair, raking it off her face. "It's going to start all over again, isn't it? The reporters, the stories."

"It already has." Hunter nodded toward the antique ivory-and-gold telephone. "I unplugged it. The calls started coming in about five minutes after Neals's suicide hit the TV." He brushed a strand of hair from her cheek with the back of his hand. "Why don't you go away for a while, Jill? Even for a couple of weeks, until the worst of it's over. You shouldn't have to go through all this again."

"I have to." She took a deep breath, closing her eyes for a second or two as though calling on a hidden reserve of strength.

Hunter frowned. "Yeah, I suppose so. Maybe the best idea is for us to just make a blanket statement, covering some of the highlights of that letter. Then we can clear your name once and for all, and get on with our lives."

"No." Jill traced the grass stain on her knee with a fingertip. She searched for the words, knowing there were no words for what she wanted to say. "I want you to forget everything I've told you, Hunter. And everything in that letter." A silence filled the room, so thick it was almost tangible. When she finally dared to look at him, Hunter was staring down at her as though disbelieving his own hearing. "Nothing will come of opening up the Phoenix business again except the ruin of a good man's reputation. Instead of being remembered for the remarkable scientist he was, he'll go down in history as a thief and a cheat."

"He was a thief and a cheat, Jill," Hunter said with strained patience, as though explaining it to a child. "What about *your* reputation? You're already famous for almost pulling off one of the most audacious and brilliant scientific frauds of modern time. You even made *Time Magazine*."

"Neals won't get a second chance to clear his name. I will."

"Damn it, Jill, the man's dead! My story can't hurt him."

"Exactly! The man *is* dead. If he was alive, at least he'd have a chance to defend himself. But this way, he'll never have an opportunity to clear his name. He did so much good, can't you see that? Print this, and it will taint everything he ever did. Everything will be suspect—his work in immunology, all his Alzheimer's research, his students, his papers. You won't be just destroying the man's name, Hunter, you'll be destroying everything he devoted his life to."

"And what about everything you've devoted your life to?" Hunter bellowed in exasperation. "He used you, Jill. Without even the slightest qualm. That's not just playing dirty, that's criminal!"

"My God, Hunter, look at you." Jill was on her feet, gesturing angrily. "Twenty minutes ago you were blaming yourself for Neals's killing himself, and now you can't wait to dance on the man's grave."

"Jill, I am not going to stand by and let you throw away the chance to clear your name because of some honorable but completely misguided sense of loyalty to your old prof. I admire your devotion to the man. I even have to admire your zeal in protecting him—you had me fooled for seven months. But that's as far as it goes. You don't owe him anything more."

"Oh, you're such a hypocrite!" Jill exploded. "Why don't you just admit the real reason you want to write this story? You're not trying to clear my name, Hunter Kincaide, you're just adding finishing touches to your own reputation!"

"Of course I want to write the story." Hunter's voice was intense. "The man gave it to me to *be* written."

"Oh, well, that makes it all right, doesn't it."

"Jill, what the hell's wrong with you?" Hunter glared down at her. "I'd have thought you'd be glad it's finally over."

"But it isn't over, Hunter, can't you see that? Not for Neals. Not for his family. He's got a couple of children, a grandson. We can't leave them a legacy like this."

"Dear God." It was more a whispered prayer than blasphemy, and Hunter stared at the ceiling as though requesting divine assistance. "Jill the Good strikes again."

"Don't be so damned sarcastic."

"Then don't be so damned naive." Hunter turned his head to give her a hard, impatient look. "This isn't Sunday school where you turn your other cheek and forgive your neighbor his trespasses. This is reality. That neighbor just ruined your life, lady! I'm going to write the story. It's time the truth about Phoenix came out once and for all."

"Truth?" Jill laughed harshly. "What do you know about truth, Hunter? One of the first rules a scientist learns is not to become part of the experiment he's watching. But that's what you do. You push and prod and pressure people, then sit back to see how they respond." She turned away. "You manipulated the situation at Phoenix to get the final answer just like Neals and DeRocher did. If you hadn't pushed Neals past his breaking point, it wouldn't have ended this way—it would have been a different *truth*."

"Don't split philosophical hairs with me, Jill," Hunter growled behind her. "I'm not in the mood. I had a story to write, and I went after it. You knew exactly what was going to happen before you turned me loose on DeRocher. You *counted* on the fact I wouldn't give up, in fact, so don't get all bent out of shape because I went a little further than you'd planned."

"A *little* further?" Jill turned to look at him. "I was trying to protect Dr. Neals, not drive him to suicide!"

Hunter's eyes darkened dangerously. "That wasn't exactly my plan, either."

"But the end always justifies the means with you, doesn't it? As long as you get an ending to your story, it doesn't matter who gets hurt." She wheeled away and stalked across the room. "They call you The Surgeon because of your skill at cutting through to the heart of the story, but you're no surgeon, Hunter. A surgeon cuts away the bad for the good of the patient, but you cut away all the good and keep the bad because it makes a better story. And you justify it to the world and yourself as investigative journalism, saying you're only bringing John Q. Public what he wants—his right to know!''

"What is it you want from me, Jill?" Hunter's eyes locked with hers. "Do you want me to lie?"

"I just want you to let the story end here. No one knows Neals sent you that letter."

"The way I look at it, manipulating the truth, or simply not telling it at all, is the same thing as telling an outright lie."

"And what do you call getting computer access using a borrowed security card?" she challenged. "You have a very flexible sense of ethics, Hunter."

"No more flexible than yours," he shot back. "Or is a sin of omission less serious than a sin of commission in your book?"

Jill drew in a deep breath for a sharp reply, then let it out again. She drew her fingers through her thick hair again. "Hunter, I don't want to fight with you. We've been over this same ground a thousand times."

Hunter stared at her mistrustfully, then some of the anger and impatience left his face. He smiled faintly. "That we have. Phoenix hasn't exactly brought out the best in us, Boston."

"No." She rubbed her bare arms. "I wish I'd never heard of the place."

"Six months from now, Jill, no one will even remember the word. You'll be working again, the scandal about Neals will all be forgotten, the Ackertons will be pouring money into the new disease of the week, and if there's any justice, DeRocher will be washing dishes in a fast-food joint." He walked across the room and slipped his arms around her, kissing the side of her throat. "Let's go out to dinner. Then I'll help you draft up a statement for the press. The island will be crawling with TV crews and reporters by morning, and the sooner you have your say, the sooner they'll leave you alone. Then I'll have to go up to Chapel Hill and get the final chapter written myself. Before some young hotshot comes along and scoops me at my own story."

Jill stepped out of his embrace, turning to look up at him. "Can't you just let it go?" she whispered, already knowing the answer.

Hunter gazed down at her, his face riven. "I'm sorry, Jill, but I can't. I'm a journalist. This is my story."

"I see." Jill turned away from him and looked out the window, seeing nothing. "Then I guess that's it."

"Jill . . ."

"Don't you ever have any doubts?" she asked, suddenly furious with him, wanting to see some emotion—any emotion—on that craggy, stubborn face.

"Yes, I have doubts," he replied very quietly. "I just don't let them get in the way."

"Of course not." She gave him a hostile look. "Everything's so black-and-white with you. You go through life being so sure of everything. Of yourself, of other people. You were sure that Neals was guilty, that I wasn't, that I loved you."

"You do." He said it unemotionally, as though they were discussing the weather or football scores. As though it was the only thing he was certain of in an uncertain world.

"It's not enough, Hunt. I'm not like you. I can't always tell absolute right from absolute wrong. I try, but sometimes I get lost between. And I . . ." She gestured helplessly. "I'm lost in there now somewhere."

"It's not really hard to tell right from wrong. You just have to listen to yourself."

"Well, maybe I'm just not as good a listener as you are." She turned away again. She felt like crying, but the tears were stuck in her throat, salty and hot. "You'd better go, Hunter," she said quietly. *Stay,* she begged him silently. *Stay and tell me you love me and that Neals's story will end here.*

"Jill . . ." The silence pulled wire taut. He breathed something under his breath and strode to the door.

He paused there with his hand on the knob and Jill thought he was going to say something. She turned expectantly, her heart giving a funny little cartwheel. But all that was there was the empty doorway, and the sound of footsteps.

"Jill!" The name, shouted so loudly and desperately from the suffocating depths of the nightmare, jolted Hunter awake. He sat up, panting for breath, his heart trip-hammering. The sheets were soaked with sweat and he'd kicked the bedding into knots sometime during those two hours of tortured sleep.

Damn it, what was happening to him? Night after night he awoke in the middle of the night with the tendrils of some terrifying nightmare clinging to him, Jill's name still on his lips. He could never quite remember what the dream was about except that he was chasing Jill, trying to catch her. He always seemed to be fighting his way through a crowd while she got farther and farther away, and he'd wake up shouting her name, sick with loss.

He swore at himself and lunged off the bed, prowling the darkness of his bedroom. *Don't you ever have any doubts?* Jill had shouted at him tonight. Hunter smiled grimly as he sat on the edge of the bed. "Hell, lady," he whispered into the darkness. "My whole world is filled with doubt lately."

It hadn't always been like that. There'd been a time when he'd never had a doubt from dawn to dusk about anything. It hadn't always earned him friends, but it had earned him respect. To be the best, that's what had kept him going. To keep working on a story long after others would have quit, to keep digging and worrying at it until it relinquished what he wanted. That tenacity had usually paid off, and knowing he'd gotten the story when thousands of others wouldn't have was intensely satisfying.

Or it used to be. The Phoenix story hadn't been like that. At times he found himself wondering who was chasing whom: was he after Phoenix, or was it after him? He'd sunk his bulldog jaws into solid flesh, but the prey was dragging him down, not the other way around. Down into a mire of doubt and confusion as thick as any in his nightmares.

And if he just let go? he brooded. If he lost his writing, what in God's name was left?

"You're nothing but words, Hunter," Vickie had screamed at him once. "There's nothing real under there, just more and more words. You say things, but you don't feel them. You write about despair and pain, but they don't touch you. You've cut yourself off from your feelings because words won't die or leave you alone or demand anything from you. But they'll never fill up that empty place inside you. There's no story or award big enough to fill that much loneliness."

Hunter lunged to his feet again, swearing. Lately those bitter little shots of Vickie's were turning up in his thoughts more and more often. Because of Phoenix? God, he was going to be glad when it was finally over and he could get on with something else.

It *was* over. He pulled open the big glass door to the bedroom balcony and stepped outside, feeling the warm, damp sea air curl around his bare ribs. The roar of the surf was very loud and he leaned his elbows on the balcony railing and stared down at the water. The Phoenix story was finished. And thanks to Neals's confession, it was going to be even better than he'd anticipated.

So why, he asked himself angrily, did he feel so depressed? He hadn't pulled the trigger of Neals's gun. And he hadn't pulled any journalistic trickery to get that letter, either. Neals had sent it to him; the story was his. The fact that Jill was all tangled up in the intricacies of right and wrong, trying to find answers to questions that hadn't even been asked, wasn't his problem. He understood loyalty. But Jill had carried her loyalty to an old professor beyond the limits of common sense. It was possible that Neals understood that better than Jill herself at the end, which would explain why he hadn't sent the letter to her. He'd have known she wouldn't release the information in it, even to clear her own name or make Simon DeRocher pay.

Hunter smiled. Jill the Good. She'd martyr herself on a bonfire of good intentions just to protect a secret Neals didn't want protected, not understanding that this was his way of seeking absolution.

And yet, he found himself asking for about the fiftieth time that night, was the fact that Jill was wrong make him more right? Or was there, as she fiercely maintained, room for doubt between the absolutes?

Oh, Jill, he thought with a trace of humor, you've turned this whole thing into a damned theological debate!

The big coconut palms along the edge of the lawn stood silhouetted like black scythes against the moon-bright sky, their ragged fronds clattering softly. They looked like sentinels out there, guarding the domain of man from the mysterious wilderness of water just beyond.

Something moved on the beach. Hunter stared at the lone figure walking slowly along the water's edge, head down, shoulders rounded in the familiar posture of Sanibel beach walkers. He smiled at his fellow insomniac and was tempted to dress and go down and join him. Maybe somewhere down there, feet washed by the gentle surf, mind on the shells at his feet, he'd find answers to some of the questions rolling around in his mind.

The lone stroller stopped and looked over the Gulf, lifting a hand to brush back a tangle of wind-teased hair. There was something in the gesture that caught Hunter's attention and he stared at the figure more closely, realizing with a little jolt that it wasn't a man at all. But it was only when the woman turned away from the Gulf and looked up at his apartment that Hunter understood.

Jill!

Ten

Hunter stared down at her in concern. What in hell was she doing walking along a deserted strip of Florida beach at two in the morning? Did she know he was up here, as restless and sleepless as she, thinking of her?

He could see her face clearly in the moonlight, and although she was too far away for him to discern her features, he could have sworn their eyes met and held. It was like a touch of electricity and he felt his pulse jump; telling himself he was crazy. There was no way she could see him. Yet, when she started walking slowly across the beach toward the building, he found he wasn't surprised.

He waited for her just inside his apartment door, not bothering to turn on any lights. He heard the elevator doors sigh open and a moment later there was a soft tap on his door. He opened it and she stepped inside, carrying the scent of the wind and sea in with her like perfume, and in the next instant she was in his arms, trembling and tasting of tears.

Her mouth was warm and nectar sweet and he took it greedily, his mind spinning. She was like wind and fire in his hands and she moved against him urgently, inflaming him with her need.

He wrenched his mouth from hers and gasped her name but she kissed him fiercely, silencing him. He realized that she didn't need words tonight; tonight she just needed him and, if only for a little while, a time and place where there was no Phoenix or Preston Neals or Simon DeRocher. Just a time and a place where no one existed but the two of them.

And that, at least, he thought with gratified wonder, was something he could give her.

It wasn't until he'd carried her into the bedroom and had undressed her that he realized she was icy cold. She lay shivering uncontrollably and he wrapped his arms around her and pulled her as close as possible, not making love to her but holding her. It wasn't the physical loving she needed just then, he knew, but the emotional kind; what she needed most was an undemanding warmth to shield her.

She clung to him and he could feel the tremors run through her in wave after wave, gradually lessening as his body warmth soaked into her. After a long while she sighed and relaxed against him. She still shivered when he ran his hand down her back and hip, but her response was different now. She moved under the caress like a stroked cat, loving his touch. She started moving her own hands, lightly at first and then with more confidence, drawing the responses from him that she knew so well.

As his caresses became more and more intimate, Jill murmured his name, her breath catching now and again until she was like hot silk beneath his fingers. He eased himself into the cradle of her thighs and as he slipped deeply into her warmth, she moaned with pleasure and gripped him fiercely with her legs.

His own pleasure was so intense he had to gasp for breath, aching with that delicious, centered tension that seemed to draw tighter and tighter until he was sure he couldn't last. Yet he managed to keep it at the very edge, drawing it out for them both until there was just a feathery tingle at the base of his spine, waiting until he felt Jill stiffen for that telltale instant.

She went motionless, not even breathing, as though afraid to go that one tiny step further. Eyes slitted, he watched her as he held her there, letting her savor the sensation. Then he took her the rest of the way, seeing for one fleeting moment the magic on her face as she arched under him with a soft, drawn-out cry, her body tightening around him so vitally that it took his own breath away.

Little electric tremors ran through her like ripples in a pond and he moved his hips again and again, just enough to keep them from dying away completely. To his satisfaction, another wave swept over her, even more intense this time, and she groaned his name and moved lithely under him, digging her fingers into the small of his back as she strove to pull him even more deeply into her. It was only then that he let go and simply enjoyed her, loving the feel of her around him, the textures and scents and tastes of her.

He lost himself to her totally, and for one heart-stopping instant he felt as though he'd stepped off the edge of the world. Dimly, he heard his own voice calling, felt Jill's slim hips rock rhythmically against his, heard her whispering his name coaxingly, and then everything vanished in a blinding uprush of pure sensation.

It seemed like hours later that he became aware of reality again, yet he knew it had been only seconds. Jill's strong legs were still wrapped around his hips and he could feel her heart pounding, realized that in those last few moments he'd grasped her rounded bottom in his hands and that his fingers were still curved urgently around her. He ran his hands up her back in a long, lingering caress. She wriggled comfortably, sighing, already half-asleep, and he opened his mouth to tell her he loved her, then decided words were a trifle redundant at that moment.

Words. The easy way out. Words were the paints he used to draw pictures in his reader's mind. They could evoke an emotion, like love, yet they were not that emotion. Love was not a word, love was...

Love was lying in his arms, sound asleep, he realized with a drowsy smile. Love still had her legs tangled with his, and love's body still held him in that last, intimate embrace. And if there were words to describe the happiness and contentment he felt, he'd yet to encounter them.

"Jill Benedict, you're going to regret this!" Kathy Fischer came racing down the corridor toward her as Jill stepped in the front door of the clinic, a bundle of file folders under one arm and a small brown dog under the other. The phone in the front office was ringing shrilly, the small dog was yapping, and from somewhere in the back an indignant cat was giving full voice to its annoyance. "It's not that I'm not glad to see you or anything, but this place has been a madhouse this morning!"

"Oh, Kath, I'm sorry." Jill tossed her big canvas shoulder bag onto a chair and grabbed one of the white lab coats out of the storage cabinet. She shook it out and pulled it on swiftly, then rescued the folders as they started to slip out of Kathy's grip. "This morning was a little...hectic."

No need to tell her, Jill decided, that she was late because Hunter had decided to join her in the shower. And that the inventive lovemaking that had ensued had taken up the better part of half an hour and had left them both so pleasantly exhausted that they'd collapsed on the thick, plush bathroom rug afterward, dripping wet and half-drowned but utterly happy. "And it took me nearly an hour and a half to get up to the post office for the mail this morning. The traffic was murder!" She set the files aside and started pulling the office mail out of the canvas bag, dumping it onto Kathy's desk by the handful.

Kathy answered the telephone in a breathless voice, holding the receiver out of the dog's reach as she strained to hear over its barking. Her mouth pulled tight and she shouted "Wrong number!" into it then slammed it down, pulling back as the dog stopped barking long enough to lick her face.

"What can I do to help?" Jill asked solicitously.

"Go home," Kathy told her emphatically. The phone started ringing again but she ignored it. "I'm serious, Jill. We've had six reporters and a TV crew here already this morning. I don't know how they found out you're working here, but I think a couple of them camped outside all night. One of them took a swing at Brett when he told them to get lost, and Brett decked him. How did you get by them at your apartment this morning?"

"I . . . uh . . . wasn't there last night," Jill admitted sheepishly.

"Oh." Kathy's eyebrows shot up, then came down again as her small freckled face broke into a huge grin. "Well, well. It's about time, if you don't mind my saying so. But you could have come in together, you know. I was single myself once."

It took Jill a moment to understand, then she gave a peal of laughter. "It's not Brett, Kathy! I mean, he's one of the sweetest men I know, and if things were different I probably wouldn't need to be invited twice, but—"

"'Sweetest man you know'?" interrupted a despairing baritone from behind her. "God, what a thing to call the

man who's been lusting after you for the past five months."
Brett came into the office with the subtlety of a blizzard, lab
coat flying behind him. He took the dog that Kathy thrust
at him and poured a cup of coffee with his free hand, casting Jill a sideways look as he added the cream. "The story
about Preston Neals is all over the front page of every
newspaper in the country, sweetheart. And every one of
those papers has a reporter outside, waiting for you to put
your nose out the door. How did you get in without getting
mobbed?"

"I came through the backyard," Jill said in confusion.
"What's happening?"

"Phoenix fever," Brett said succinctly. He handed the
dog to her and headed toward the back again, sipping his
coffee on the run. "Interested in taking a canoe trip out into
the middle of a mangrove swamp for the day?"

"Yes! What am I doing with this dog, by the way?"

"What dog?" Brett looked around as though seeing it for
the first time. "Who does it belong to?"

"I don't know. You gave it to me."

"I did?" He looked surprised. "Damned if I know. Ask
Kath."

Kathy appeared just then, looking harried, and Jill
handed the dog to her. She took it absently and handed Jill
a handful of pink telephone messages in return. "These are
some of the people who have called you this morning. The
rest were calling en route from somewhere and said they'd
call back." She looked at the dog in confusion. "What am
I supposed to do with this? I thought you wanted to keep
him overnight to see how the antibiotics work."

"I did?" Brett looked at the dog again.

"Honestly, Brett, don't you ever hear anything I say?"
Kathy walked across and popped the little dog into one of
the floor kennels. "Mrs. Sutherland called last night and

said she was bringing it in. One of Iris Carruthers's cats laid its ear open and it got infected.''

"The same one that swallowed all the knitting wool?" Jill pointed to the half-grown tom glaring out of its cage at them. It saw the dog and set into a high-decibel yowl, eyes like pools of lava. The dog gave a terrified yelp and bolted to the back of its small kennel, and Jill laughed. "Looks like we're in for an interesting couple of days."

"I need a vacation," Brett groaned. "What do you say to forgetting the canoe trip and taking the *Sweet Retreat* down to the Caribbean for about six months?"

"Don't tempt me," Jill said with a matching groan as she leafed through the telephone messages. "I don't believe this!"

"Believe it. That phone's been ringing since seven this morning with people wanting to talk with you."

"Kath, I'm sorry." Jill wadded up the entire stack of messages and tossed them into a nearby trash basket. "Maybe I should go home. There's no point in keeping both of you from getting anything done just because—"

"Forget it," Brett interrupted firmly. "You're not going anywhere unless Kincaide or I are with you, got that? These guys are ready to kill to get a story. Or get killed." He flexed his right hand, looking at his knuckles reflectively.

"My God, you didn't really hit that reporter this morning, did you?" Jill looked at him in horror.

Brett smiled a slow, satisfied smile. "Laid him out like a deck of cards."

"Brett, you idiot! He'll probably sue you within an inch of your life."

"I doubt that." The smile grew even more satisfied. "Chief of Police Dexter's a good friend of mine. I saved a golden labrador of his that got mixed up with that old one-eyed 'gator that lives behind Bailey's. And I used to go out with his daughter now and again, until she married a good-for-nothing lawyer from Tampa.''

"You mean the good-for-nothing lawyer who built her a six bedroom house in Fort Myers Beach?" Kathy asked innocently. "The one who's planning to run for Governor next year?"

"That's the one," Brett growled. "The only thing more dishonest than a lawyer is a politician."

"Kincaide? Did you say something about a Kincaide?" Kathy rummaged through the roomy pockets in her smock. "There was a guy here this morning who said his name was Kincaide. He wanted to give you something, but you weren't here."

"Hunter?" Jill looked at Kathy in surprise. "But I was just talking with him two hours ago."

"Yeah, I know. He was hoping to find you here, but when I told him you always stop off to pick up the mail on your way in, he left this." She pulled a manila envelope out of her pocket and handed it to Jill triumphantly. "Knew it was in there!"

"Why didn't he wait?" Jill asked in bewilderment.

A distant phone started ringing and Kathy headed for the door. "Said something about having to catch a plane to Washington."

Now what? Jill's stomach pulled tight as she opened the envelope and peered inside, recognizing Dr. Neals's letter. She and Hunter hadn't mentioned a word about Neals or the letter or anything else even vaguely associated with Phoenix Research this morning.

But reality had to intrude sometime, Jill reminded herself glumly as she pulled the sheets of paper from the envelope. Hunter hadn't said a thing about leaving for Washington this morning. He obviously hadn't wanted to spoil things for her, and that could only mean he was going back to finish his Phoenix story. And *that* meant . . . what?

That was just one of the bewildering questions that had kept her mind in a turmoil all night. And she was no closer to an answer now than she'd been at two this morning when she'd wound up walking on the beach, trying to outrun the nightmares.

Hunter had attached a brief note to the letter, and she frowned as she tried to decipher his untidy scrawl.

Think this is yours, Boston. You got away this morning before I could give it to you. I don't agree with you—hell, you already know that—but I also don't want to lose you. Got a call this a.m. that all hell's busting loose at Phoenix & Co. Think I should be there to keep the lid on things until you've decided what you want people to know about Neals. But whatever you decide, it's all right with me. Story or no story, I love you. It's your call, kid.

Beneath the note was a row of little hearts.

"Oh, damn you, Kincaide," Jill whispered, her eyes swimming. "Just when I think I've got you figured out, and you go and do something like this."

"Kincaide giving you trouble?" Brett rumbled.

"No." Jill gulped, trying to laugh and cry at the same time and doing both badly. "How would you like to come to a wedding, Brett?"

"Only if I get to kiss the bride."

Jill laughed up at him through tears. "You could kiss me right now if you don't mind getting soaked."

Brett bent down and kissed her gently on the mouth, his rain-blue eyes filled with laughter. "I've been known to be a sore loser, sweetheart, but if he makes you happy enough to cry, I guess I'll have to back down gracefully.''

"I love the man," Jill told him simply, wiping her cheeks with the back of her hand.

"You know," Brett said dreamily, gazing down at her, "you've almost made me believe there is such a thing. Never thought a renegade bachelor like me would catch himself saying a thing like this, but lately I've found myself wondering what it would be like to settle down." Then he grinned broadly, breaking the mood. "On the other hand, it could be just a temporary mental aberration."

"Jill!" Kathy's voice came fluting down the corridor. "Phone. I don't think you want to miss this one."

"Hunter!" Jill sprang toward the door, laughing. "Back in a minute, Renegade."

But it wasn't Hunter. Jill listened to the quiet, matter-of-fact voice on the other end of the line with a frown that got progressively deeper as the minutes passed. When she set the receiver back in its cradle, she stared at it thoughtfully. "Strange."

"Really?" Kathy was going through the mail, only half-listening. "She sounded normal enough."

"The call, not the caller. It was Dr. Mary Couzinet."

Kathy's head shot up. "*That* Dr. Mary Couzinet? She said it had something to do with the Ethics Committee hearings, but she didn't bother saying she was heading it up!"

"One and the same." Jill's frown deepened. "She says they want me back up there next week to testify again."

"Because of Dr. Neals's death?"

"Yes." Jill looked at her. "New evidence has been presented to the Commission that . . . changes things."

"Changes? What evidence? And what kind of changes?"

Jill shook her head. "I don't know. She wouldn't give me any details, just said that it looks like I'll be back at work by Christmas."

"Oh, Jill. That's wonderful!" Kathy said, dropping the letter she'd been opening.

"The letter!"

"What letter?" Kathy, startled, looked down at her desk.

"This letter." Jill pulled Dr. Neals's confession out of the pocket of her lab coat. "My God, Kathy, he sent a copy to the Ethics Review Committee!" She stared at the other woman in shock.

Kathy looked totally bewildered by now. "Am I supposed to know what you're talking about?" she asked cautiously.

"No." Jill looked down at the letter in her hand almost reverently. "No, Kathy, I'm sorry. It's just that this is all so confusing and . . . unexpected." Then she suddenly thought of something else. "I have to find Hunter right now!" She tore her lab coat off and flung it aside. "What flight was he catching, did he say? When did he leave here? Was he heading back to his apartment, or—"

"He was heading over to Fort Myers from here, I think. He left maybe thirty minutes ago."

"Half an hour." Jill bit her lower lip, looking up at the big wall clock. "The traffic's unbelievable on Periwinkle this morning. There's no way he'd have gotten to the causeway yet."

She grabbed her bag and started for the door, then paused and came flying back to Kathy's desk. Snatching up the receiver, she swiftly dialed the emergency number. As Kathy's eyes got wider and wider, Jill hastily gave the police dispatcher a description of Hunter's rental car, the license number and an even hastier description of Hunter himself. "He's got a small scar on his chin, and a bite mark on—

well, never mind that. What? No, he's not dangerous. Just make sure someone stops him before he gets on the causeway. What's he done?" Jill looked at Kathy for help. "He's stolen something," she said impulsively. "Yes, he's definitely stolen something."

"Jill!" Kathy followed her as she ran out the door. "Are you all right?"

"I'm fine!" Jill called back. Three men sitting in their air-conditioned cars stared at her curiously. Then, as one, they flung the doors open and started after her, shouting questions. She dodged them and slipped behind the wheel of her own car, slamming the door closed so swiftly one of the reporters very nearly lost his fingers. She grinned and waved merrily as she wheeled the car out of the driveway, spraying gravel. "Sorry, guys," she called, not caring they couldn't hear her. "This is Hunt's story!"

"I can not believe you did that." Hunter strode across the parking lot toward Jill's car, his feet crunching through the crushed shell and coral. "I can't believe you'd actually have me arrested."

"I didn't have you arrested!" Jill had to practically run to keep up with him, biting her lip to keep from laughing. "I just wanted to catch you, and calling the police seemed like the easiest way to do it."

Hunter stopped at the car and turned to look down at her. "He was serious about charging you with public mischief, you know. If Douglass hadn't turned up when he did, we'd both be behind bars."

"He didn't seem to have much of a sense of humor, did he?" Jill looked up at him, trying to keep the laughter out of her eyes. "Hunt, I'm sorry."

He looked only slightly mollified, and in all honesty Jill couldn't blame him. Calling the police out to set up a roadblock at the island end of the causeway hadn't been the brightest thing she'd ever done. And Police Chief Nelson Dexter had been only too happy to point that fact out to her. In fact, she was still smarting from the lecture she'd gotten from Dexter, followed closely by one from Brett and a third from Hunter himself.

"It's a wonder they're not running us out of town on a rail," Hunter was muttering. "The sooner I get you off this island and into Washington, the safer we'll all be."

"You make me sound like the mad woman of Chaillot."

"You've been acting like the mad woman of Chaillot," Hunter told her bluntly. "They never did tell me what you'd accused me of stealing."

"I didn't tell them." She smiled brightly at him. "You stole my heart, you bandit. But I didn't think Chief Dexter was in any mood to appreciate the joke."

"I should strangle you on the spot," Hunter murmured, slipping his hands around her throat in a loving caress and tugging her toward him.

"In front of the police station, darling?"

"They'd put it down to justifiable homicide and tell me I should stick to women with huge breasts and small IQs instead of the other way around—ow!"

Jill untangled her fists from his hair and smiled sweetly. "I don't remember you complaining about the ratio before."

"You never had me arrested before." Hunter kissed her soundly. "Instead of strangling you, maybe I'll just drag you back to my apartment and force my attentions on you all afternoon."

"Mmm," Jill murmured against his mouth. "That sounds like suitable punishment. Promise?"

Hunter laughed as he pulled the car door open. "You are turning into a woman of strong sexual appetites, my love.

Quite a far cry from the scared little virgin I led trembling to my bed seven months ago.''

"I wasn't a virgin," she reminded him as she slid into the car. But in spite of herself, she had to smile. "Technically, at any rate." She looked at him, smile widening. "I was pretty awful, wasn't I? Before you turned the light off, I didn't know where to look. After you turned it off, I didn't know what to do. I was terrified you'd expect a virtuoso performance when I hadn't even learned my scales properly.''

Hunter gave a peal of laughter. "Surprising what regular practice will do for you." He closed the door and walked around to the passenger side. "You're playing chauffeur, by the way. Dexter promised he'd have my rental dropped off at the apartment later. I think he wants to check it out for a stash of cocaine or dirty magazines or something.''

Jill waited until he was settled, then turned and took one of his hands between hers. "Thank you, Hunt," she said softly.

"For?"

"Preston Neals." She met his gaze. "I know how much finishing that Phoenix story meant to you, Hunter. Finishing it properly, I mean." She stroked the back of his hand with her fingertips. "When I had to leave the Phoenix team with my MS project only half-finished, I felt as though a part of me were incomplete. For weeks, I'd wake up every morning with my mind spinning with the things I had to do, then I'd remember . . .''

Hunter put his fingers under her chin and gently lifted her face. "It's not the story that makes me whole, Jill. It's you. It's taken me seven months to realize that. This morning, after you left my apartment, I knew I couldn't use Neals's letter and confession in the wrap-up to my series. I might not understand why you're doing it, but if you want Neals's past to die with him, then that's the way it'll be. I'll live without it. But I don't want to think about living without you."

"Write the story." Jill watched Hunter's eyes grow puzzled. "I got a phone call this morning from the head of the Ethics Review Committee. New evidence has come in that clears me unconditionally of the Phoenix fraud, and I have to go up there on Monday and testify again. Dr. Couzinet wouldn't say what evidence they'd received, except that it had something to do with Neals's suicide." She heard Hunter suck in his breath and nodded. "The letter. That's all it can be. He sent it to you because he didn't trust me. Maybe he sent a copy to the Ethics Committee because he didn't entirely trust you, either."

"What are you going to tell them?"

He asked the question so gently that it took Jill a moment to understand. Then she smiled raggedly. "The black-and-white truth, Hunter. I'll probably get a good rap on the knuckles for not screaming my head off when I first suspected what DeRocher was up to. And they sure as heck aren't going to appreciate the fact I went to *you* with the story and not them."

"They'll be so busy going after DeRocher they'll forget all about you."

"She asked me if I wanted a job," Jill mused. "She's a lab director at the National Institutes of Health and she seemed interested in my work."

"It's going to be rough for the next few weeks, you realize that, don't you?" he asked gently. "The media's going to stick to you like burrs."

"That's why I want you to write the story. Everybody's going to have a field day with it, not getting a damned thing straight, and I want it written right—for his sake." Hunter hesitated, and Jill smiled, lifting his hand to her mouth and kissing each knuckle in turn. "The truth, Hunter. All of it. But I hope with a touch of humanity."

Hunter smiled at her. "I've been doing a lot of thinking about that, too. And maybe you're right. Maybe there are times when that black-and-white truth blurs to gray. Maybe that's what compassion is all about, knowing when to see the blur."

"I don't know, Hunt." She stared out the windshield, still cradling his hand between hers. "I don't know if I'm any closer to the answers. Dr. Neals did so many good things even while doing the bad. I lied to you and, indirectly, to the Ethics people for what I thought was a good reason—to protect Dr. Neals. Does that make me good, bad, or just gullible? Can you tally rights and wrongs and come up with a figure, I wonder?"

"Maybe we're not even supposed to try." Hunter squeezed her fingers. "Maybe we're not supposed to have all the answers, Jill. Just as a reminder that none of us is perfect."

Jill winced. "Don't ever say that to a scientist, Kincaide. Our whole lives are dedicated to nothing *but* finding all the answers." Then she laughed. "I bet if we went back in there and asked Police Chief Dexter the definition of right and wrong he'd be able to give it to us, chapter and verse."

"I have a feeling he'd just as soon toss us in jail as discuss metaphysical conundrums," Hunter growled. "We don't have to solve all of life's mysteries this morning, Jill. Let's leave a couple for next week."

"Such as where we're going to live when this is all over. I'll be finished my work here in another month, and by then Aunt Steph and Uncle Roland will want their condo back for a few weeks. Got a spare room in that Washington town house of yours?"

"For you, no." Hunter smiled. "You'll have to share a room."

"With the lord of the manor?" Jill purred.

"For as long as you want."

"How about forever? That offer you made about making an honest woman of me still hold?"

Hunter's eyes met hers in surprise. "Are you serious? You mean you've changed your mind about waiting?"

"I've wasted seven months of happiness, Hunter, and seven months of research time. I want to go up to Bethesda and take this job with Couzinet and get on with my work—and I want to get married and make babies and play house." She smiled. "Think I can handle all that?"

"I think you can handle anything you put your mind to, Jill Benedict." He kissed her lightly. "Bethesda's nice and close to Washington. We could keep the town house."

"We could."

"It's got three bedrooms and a den."

"An office for you and an office for me and a third for some little Kincaides."

"And the fourth as a laboratory for brewing up those little Kincaides in the first place."

"You have a one-track mind. And I thought you didn't approve of my 'brewing up' children."

"I was thinking of a mutual brewing, my love." He settled his mouth over hers in a long, drugging kiss that sent little tingling shocks through her. The hand hidden by their bodies caressed her breast until Jill gave a little gasping laugh and pulled away.

"You're going to get us arrested again!"

"We're probably the most fun these guys have had in weeks," Hunter chuckled. "Kiss me."

She did, until they were both breathless. "Thank you."

"You're welcome."

"I don't mean just for this, you idiot," Jill protested, removing his hand from her thigh. "I mean for everything. For coming down here after all the awful things I said in Chapel Hill. For staying after all the awful things I've said here. For giving me the time I needed to put things in perspective and understand that what happened at Phoenix didn't have anything to do with you and me—or how I feel about you. It would have been so easy for you to have just given up, and we'd never have had this second chance. I'd never have had the chance to say I'm sorry, or tell you how much I love you."

"Is Douglass expecting you back at the clinic right away?"

"What did you have in mind?"

"Taking you home and letting you tell me how much you love me in more detail." He kissed her again. "And if he asks, you can tell him you were home playing with your chemistry set or something."

"Chemistry?" Jill asked with a gasp of laughter.

"Pure chemistry," Hunter assured her. "Nitro and glycerin, remember?"

* * * * *

Silhouette Desire

COMING NEXT MONTH

#391 BETRAYED BY LOVE—Diana Palmer
Kate had loved Jacob forever, but he had always considered her off limits. She couldn't risk telling him her true feelings—but then Jacob started taking some risks of his own....

#392 RUFFLED FEATHERS—Katherine Granger
Cass was sure that Ryan's interest in her was strictly business. He was playing with her heart to get her uncle's secret recipe. But one look at Cass and Ryan knew he was playing for keeps.

#393 A LUCKY STREAK—Raye Morgan
Kelly's life was secure until she rescued gambler Cash Angeli from a gang of thugs. They were from different worlds, but together they found a lifelong lucky streak.

#394 A TASTE OF FREEDOM—Candice Adams
When Felicity met Clark, she knew immediately he was a man with a past. She was shocked when she discovered his secret, but then it was too late—he'd already stolen her heart.

#395 PLAYING WITH MATCHES—Ariel Berk
Adrienne's business was matchmaking, but she was *always* mistaken when it came to herself. When she fell for Scott she knew he must be all wrong, but Scott was determined to change her mind!

#396 TWICE IN A LIFETIME—BJ James
Stonebridge was a quiet place to recuperate for Gabe—but when Caroline fell off the roof and into his arms, rest was the last thing on his mind.

AVAILABLE NOW:

#385 LADY BE GOOD
Jennifer Greene

#386 PURE CHEMISTRY
Naomi Horton

#387 IN YOUR WILDEST DREAMS
Mary Alice Kirk

#388 DOUBLE SOLITAIRE
Sara Chance

#389 A PRINCE OF A GUY
Kathleen Korbel

#390 FALCON'S FLIGHT
Joan Hohl

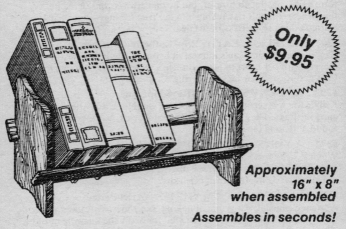

COMING NEXT MONTH

Silhouette Classics

**The best books from the past by
your favorite authors.**

The first two stories of a delightful collection...

#1 DREAMS OF EVENING by Kristin James

As a teenager, Erica had given Tonio Cruz all her love, body and soul,
but he betrayed and left her anyway. Ten years later, he was back in her
life, and she quickly discovered that she still wanted him. But the
situation had changed—now she had a son. A son who was very much
like his father, Tonio, the man she didn't know whether to hate—or love.

#2 INTIMATE STRANGERS by Brooke Hastings

Rachel Grant had worked hard to put the past behind her, but Jason
Wilder's novel about her shattered her veneer of confidence. When they
met, he turned her life upside down again. Rachel was shocked to
discover that Jason wasn't the unfeeling man she had imagined. Haunted
by the past, she was afraid to trust him, but he was determined to write a
new story about her—one that had to do with passion and tenderness
and love.